MW00329932

Mystery

of

MaryAnne

David DeVowe

His Visible Hand Books
See God's hand in *your* life.

Copyright © 2016 His Visible Hand Books
All rights reserved.

Scripture quotations are taken from The Authorized (King James) Version of the Holy Bible, which is in the Public Domain.

For the invisible things of him from the creation of the
world are clearly seen…
–Romans 1:20

Contents

ACKNOWLEDGMENTS

Cover design: Michael DeVowe Creative Works
Cover illustration: Hannah Firezar

1

Haunting Memory

The old house stood vacant eleven months and three cold days. I should know. I deserted the place nearly a year ago, as Mrs. Krebbs faltered on the eve of her death. How could MaryAnne and I forget?

Sure, the old woman was distressed over the letter from Isaac Borg. I'm certain that her age-old memories that had been tucked away since last century were of no help—not to Mrs. Krebbs. But for MaryAnne and me, her memories were tremendous help indeed—pivotal clues to the discovery of Isaac's buried treasure. It was something that only happened in dreams. I suppose that's why we hardly noticed when Mrs. Krebbs sank back into her chair, just before we passed through her front door one last time.

That spring day still haunted me. I stood in front of the dwelling, blowing on my icy fingers as evening's shadows fully engulfed the aging place. Its dark form captivated my spirit, as it did many a night on my return from trapping. Perhaps that's why I stood on the same ground where the only hearse in Stoney Creek had parked, to take one brief, final rest before finishing the trek home. Even with Mrs. Krebbs gone, her presence gripped me as if she stood in her front garden chatting with her flowers and telling me about God.

I hated that. Still, I missed her.

I suppose there was another reason I stopped in front of Mrs. Krebbs' house each night as darkness approached. It was because Mrs. Krebbs hadn't completely gone. Memories of her emerged that spring of 1926 like new stones protruding from Isaac's field, pushed forth by spring's frost. The elderly woman, who was now dead, presented herself in words and phrases from the mouth of MaryAnne. Even now, it's hard to explain. But it was as if the aged inhabited the young. It wasn't that MaryAnne was old, though far more mature than most girls at twelve. It was how she spoke.

We had been friends for two years. Unlikely friends, to be sure, and strained at times. But friends forged from having experienced more than a couple of normal adolescents ought to have. Thing was, MaryAnne wasn't normal. And her presence had changed my innocent years to anything but normal. In fact, it was MaryAnne who upset our school year to redefine what *change* was to me. There was the time that she stared down Buffalo Alice's wrath with nary a flinch as my hands trembled in my trousers. I would never forget the tears MaryAnne shed for the same Buffalo Alice as we watched Buffalo's Ma and Pa get handcuffed and then hauled off to the clink as sirens wailed and shots rang out—even as fireworks from the Fourth of July still sparkled in the night. If it weren't for MaryAnne, I would never have crouched in the bushes at the Hawthorne's drive to witness the most tumultuous event in the history of Stoney Creek.

It was MaryAnne's tears that still seared me. When she cried, stuck in a maple tree at our fort by the creek, I figured it must be what scared girls do. But the tears at Hawthorn's mansion were different, sparkling red from the crimson reflection of the sheriff's light. Tears for Buffalo Alice. No one *talked* to Buffalo Alice, let alone shed tears for her. That would have been enough to hold my interest in the uncanny person of MaryAnne. But her intent pursuit of a buried treasure, no one—including me—thought existed, entangled me in discovering just what she was all about. It was later that I discovered that MaryAnne's true passion for the treasure was not the gold and silver sealed inside the chest, it was what MaryAnne called "the most beautiful love story" that changed my grandma in ways that folks still marvel at. I know Mom and Dad loved me. But Grandma extended love to me when, after years of disinterest, Grandma became new.

MaryAnne's pursuit of the treasure led me there. How she understood its importance—at the risk of our very lives—I may never know. She tried to explain it to me more

than once. It's about church, it's about Jesus . . . That's how
the DuPrees were—churchy all the time, and preachy
sometimes, when I would rather have kept those things for
Sunday. It was the same kind of talk Mrs. Krebbs would
give me when I'd ventured by her yard. Most times I took
the long way around just to avoid it. Now that Mrs. Krebbs
wasn't around, MaryAnne had taken up the chorus, full
throated, it seemed.

I warned MaryAnne more than once when Mrs. Krebbs
was alive—how she got creepy, spouting off like Mrs.
Krebbs did. Now that the widow was gone, MaryAnne
resonated with her all the more. Creepy as it was,
MaryAnne's mimicry couldn't have been all bad, seeing
how Mrs. Krebbs managed to draw an enormous crowd to a
funeral. But it was strange—like the two of them had the
same insides. Or like Mrs. Krebbs was a part of MaryAnne.
Whatever it was, it troubled me. Though I couldn't put my
finger on it nor lay my eyes on its presence, it was there all
the same. I sensed that folks at Stoney Creek couldn't see
what was queer about Mrs. Krebbs or the red-headed
DuPree, either. So I resolved that night to solve the mystery
of MaryAnne.

With a new fortitude, I adjusted both straps that cut
deep into my shoulders. Thick canvas strained under the
weight of two dead beaver snugged headfirst into my pack.
Pond water from their cold, wet bodies soaked through my
coat, chilling me at every stop—a hefty reminder of how

well the trapping season had gone. And it was only half over.

I suppose if Dad knew how far upstream I laid my trap line, he would have me pull the whole lot. Snuffy thought he owned the South Branch. I knew better. Snuffy wasn't his real name. His real name was Clem. But like most everyone in the Upper Peninsula, Snuffy went by his nickname. Even while the memory of Snuffy's gunshots from last summer's run-in rang vividly in my head, I weighed the risk, and somewhere along the way I'd determined that trapping the upper South Branch was worth it. Anyone else might have thought me crazy. After all, my first foray onto "Snuffy's land" brought a bullet deathly close to grazing my scalp. It sounded that way. Still, I considered it a warning shot. If he had been serious about hurting me or MaryAnne, or Ricky, I reasoned, he could have done it when we returned to dig on that same land for treasure.

Perhaps the decision to trap on risky land grew on me slowly. The farther upstream I ventured, the more productive my line became. Beaver plugs and sturdy houses were built every 100 yards or so where poplar trees stood thick. And handsome beaver filled my traps. With each new catch, I dared to make another set on the dam upstream. Every new set became another exciting challenge.

Checking traps, no matter where they were set, was enough to race my pulse. Checking traps near Snuffy's squatting ground built excitement to a frenzy within me.

Each new beaver from Snuffy's claimed territory became a thrilling win. An addictive, thrilling win—reparation for his mistreatment of me and MaryAnne.

I thought it better that Dad didn't know where the best of the beaver were coming from. He and Mom had enough on their hands with Ricky, now seven, and Sophie, just old enough to have burned her finger on her first birthday candle. Besides, Snuffy hadn't shown his face in months, and was probably no more than an imagined threat to a boy of nearly fourteen.

Hardly an evening passed that I returned home with an empty pack, I thought as I readied to leave Mrs. Krebbs' yard. I reached behind with both hands, leaned forward, and then pushed up on the bottom of the wet bag until the weight of both beavers rested high on my torso. Arched over, neck extended like a hunchback who had lost his way, I glanced once more at the darkened house. What caught my eye froze me as stiff as the dead beaver chilling my spine. A dim yellow light flickered in the deceased woman's kitchen window.

I blamed my tired eyes momentarily. Still, the light lingered on the glass that Mrs. Krebbs gazed through prior to her death. I craned my neck to see what caused the reflection from behind. There was nothing but brush there. I don't know what I expected to see—the woods were as dark as night. Rotating my sight toward the house again, I caught a final glimpse of the light from inside. And then it was gone. I statued a moment longer, straining to see what had been. The more I gazed, the more untrustworthy my eyes became. Had pondering about MaryAnne and the old woman caused my imagination to play tricks on me? Or was the ghost of Mrs. Krebbs still inside?

2

Nuts!

"Is there such a thing as a real ghost?"

Mom's potato masher stopped mid-crush as she looked up from the paper beside the stove. "No, I don't think so, Shoe. Why do you ask?"

"Because I thought I saw a light, like a candle flickering, in Mrs. Krebbs' window on the way home."

"Sure you weren't seeing things?" Mama asked disinterestedly as she continued mashing. She turned back to reading the daily paper, folded open on the kitchen counter.

"Ghosts!" Ricky's tongue pushed through the gap where his front teeth had been. It glistened red between ruby lips, still bright as a girl's, though he was seven, and lips nearly as crimson as the favorite red shirt he had on. Ricky kneeled on his wooden chair, leaning toward me for emphasis. "Real ghosts? Like this?" He formed claws at the side of his bulging eyes and bared his fangs like a vampire bat.

"Knock it off," I said with measured disinterest, enough to sag Ricky into his seat.

Dad limped in from the front room, looking mighty hungry after another heavy day of lifting at the mill. "Dinner almost ready?"

Mom paused from mashing to glare at Dad. "You can't rush perfection," she teased. "Listen to this, Toivo, '*Early Release of Inmates from Asylum Prepares Facility for Newcomers.*'"

Dad didn't flinch. "What should I do with that?" he asked.

"Just sharing the news," replied Mom, mashing harder than before and speaking into the pot. "Don't you find it interesting that our state's insane population has grown to the point that an asylum has to let some go, just to manage them all?"

"Hardly a topic for dinner, Margaret."

Mom made it a habit to read the paper right before dinner—that is, if we got one. The *Peninsula Daily Gazette* was the first regular newspaper Stoney Creek had, and Mom was one of the first to get a regular copy. I often wondered if there was enough happening in our northwoods to print a paper, and one with such a pompous title. But it seemed as long as someone told something to somebody, and a person died and needed an obituary, it was enough to make a paper, and it couldn't pass for gossip anymore.

Anything in the *Peninsula Daily Gossip*, as I heard Mr. DuPree call it once, was fodder for Mom. News was news, no matter how small. Or old. "Daily" was not a good description of the newspaper, printed in a town I hadn't heard of before. The *Gazette* showed up most days, a day or two late—if it came at all. Still, as long as it was new to the Makinen household, it was news to Mom.

A headline about crazy people on the loose was enough to invigorate Mom for days—even if the *Peninsula Daily Gazette* didn't show up for another week.

"Do you think we should be concerned?" asked Mom.

"Where's this asylum you're talking about . . . and how old is that paper?" The headline was magnetic enough to give Dad pause, even between hunger and dinnertime.

"The paper's only three days old, Toivo," Mom said with conviction to support the paper's validity. "Sounds like they released about 35 inmates a couple weeks ago, from . . . let's see now." Mom studied the paper with purposed intent. "From the Northern Michigan Asylum—in Traverse City." She pursed at Dad with a slight nod to affirm to all of us that Mom was in the know. "They're saying these ones were the best suited for release, to carry on by themselves without living in a nuthouse."

"Now, Margaret," Dad interrupted, "the children." Dad furrowed at Mom, who bit her bottom lip. Then he continued, "Traverse City is hardly northern Michigan. The name of the place is a misnomer—Northern Michigan Asylum. Traverse City has to be more than 300 miles south and east of here. A good 2-day trip, driving with plenty of spares—and then there's crossing the straits on a ferry. People down there don't know the half of Michigan that's actually north."

Mom swallowed hard and raised her brow as if ready to speak, but Dad spied the cue and didn't let her in.

"It's not news when it has no effect on us. Besides, like I said, that's not a topic for dinner."

"Shoe, pour the milk," Mom said sternly.

I ate my potatoes and dry chicken legs, cooked through and through, the way Mom always did them, in silence. Only Sophie had anything to say, which none of us understood. I ignored her, and pondered Traverse City. It was a place I'd heard of a time or two before, but somehow it had more meaning than just another city in Lower Michigan. As I washed down parched chicken with a glass of milk, the scene flashed back to me. We were walking to school together that first spring the DuPrees moved to Stoney Creek when MaryAnne asked if I ever wished I lived in a different town. That's when she told me she used to live in Traverse City.

We nearly made it through supper without broaching Mom's topic. I was looking forward to asking MaryAnne if she ever saw the funny farm in Traverse City when Ricky shattered our peace.

"What's a sylum?"

Dad pushed over-boiled green beans onto his fork while his brow reached toward Ricky. "It's a hospital, Ricky."

Ricky processed that for a moment, then with a look of concern, "Does Mrs. Nomer have to take care of everybody?"

Dad stopped eating. "Mrs. Nomer? What are you talking about, Ricky?"

"You said that sylum was named for Mrs. Nomer."

Dad's brow dropped. His chicken-greased lips broke into a wide grin. Fork and knife still in hand, Dad leaned away from the table and worked up a hearty laugh. Ricky pushed back in his chair, visibly offended.

When Dad caught his breath, he said, "A misnomer, Ricky. I said the name of the place was a misnomer—that means misapplied . . . something like *confusing*. You had us *all* confused there for a minute, Richard!"

I began to chuckle. Soon, we all laughed uproariously, including Ricky, who had a way of bringing levity where it was needed the most.

***

The downside to beaver season was that a school day wouldn't end, except when Axel Crossjaw showed up. Axel's attendance was hit or miss. That's because he lived far enough in the woods to make it a journey just to get to school, if he made it at all. His ma blamed the distance from school for why Axel flunked two grades into ours. Eighth-graders were glad to see him go, and our seventh grade was loathe to welcome him, for a number of reasons that had us all keeping our distance.

Axel wore the same clothes every day, just a different layer on top. Seems he wore everything he owned, every day. Never misplaced any clothing that way. Axel was known to fight if he deemed the cause just. There was no tellin' what cause was just until Axel's long arms swung boney, scarred fists at another boy about to suffer his due. Axel lived in a house with a dirt floor, folks said. Anything known about the Crossjaw family was hearsay, because nobody we knew had actually seen their place except from a long distance. Axel's pa wasn't one for hospitality, always wielded a shotgun for supper and for protection, so they'd say. When Axel did show up for class it was worth watchin'. He'd fake learnin', then put all of his assignments in the satchel that came with him to school each day.

Axel never left his satchel. It went everywhere he did, slung over his head, strap on one shoulder, with the bag under the other arm. A few Indian-looking tassels remained on the front flap that was stained darker than the rest of the leather bag. Rumor had it that Axel's satchel held everything from knives, to mink hides, to teeth extracted from the biggest bear north of the straits. Axel's satchel, worn thin from continuous use, was clearly not holding schoolbooks most days. Near as I could tell by watching what went in and out of it, the satchel held papers Axel got assigned that day, one broken pencil, and whatever he might have brought to eat, which wasn't much.

Axel's younger brothers, Toric and Borin, more boisterous than Axel, spent much of their time either fighting or in the principal's office. So when the Crossjaws were at school there was much to pay attention to beyond the day's lessons, like the time Toric hurled a rock through a window of the girls' locker room while his 4th-grade class, outside on recess, gaped past the opening in the glass. I guess they had much to watch through the open window since sixth-grade gym had just gotten over. Screams echoed the hallways until the girls, now mostly clad, escaped the mayhem into the gym and spilled into the hallway. If we hadn't been on break between lessons, every classroom would have had to cease learning just to investigate the alarm. Since that wasn't the case, boys gawked as girls shrieked from broken glass and the rock from Toric.

The school day that passed most quickly was the day that Axel didn't come with his satchel. All the clothes were there; shirts over his wool sweater, the soiled red plaid on top. Appeared to be four layers. No telling what was underneath the sweater. But no satchel. Axel without his leather bag was remarkable enough, but he didn't have it with him because Axel had something else to carry. It was a rusty green toolbox, lookin' like it had been through the war. Probably had. There was sure to be a story about the rusty toolbox, if only we could wrench it from Axel. Being in seventh grade, we were long past show-and-tell, so the sight of Axel's toolbox got lots of attention from the moment first hour ended.

"What's the toolbox for, Axel?" Mark asked in the hallway after first hour. Axel glowered at Mark without a word. The box went with Axel to the next class and the next, never leaving his side. Few dared inquire why Axel brought the box to school, fearing more than a glower. Fourth hour was upon us when Mr. Penski, our science teacher, spied the box in the back of the room next to Axel's desk.

"Axel, what did you bring the toolbox for?" Mr. Penski asked, craning his neck as he leaned a palm on his own desk. Apparently Mr. Penski didn't want to venture any closer to Axel and his toolbox than us kids. Nobody ever sidled up to Axel on purpose.

"Axel what's in the toolbox?" Mr. Penski repeated after no reply.

"Nothin'," Axel responded, barely loud enough for the rest of us to hear. Mr. Penski, our most adventurous teacher, wasn't easily swayed.

"Oh, come on, Axel. You brought the box to school for something. Show us what's in it!"

I turned back to see what Axel would do. Axel leaned over and white-knuckled the toolbox handle, lookin' to run, near as I could tell.

"Come on. Bring the box up front so you can show us what you brought."

Axel stood up, box in hand, motionless for a moment. Then with long, slow strides he carried the toolbox to the front of the room, then set it on the floor with a metallic thunk, right in front of Mr. Penski's desk.

Mr. Penski remained planted where he was as Axel stared him down. The two stood motionless until Axel kneeled at the side of the toolbox, loosened both rusty clasps, then, at arm's length, flipped open the lid.

Out hopped a porcupine. A live porcupine, tail quills ready to strike.

I sat upright, having seen what a porcupine could do. Watching Dad pull two quills from Oscar's tongue was all the porcupine experience I needed. I also had seen how much provoking Oscar had to give the porcupine before the lightning speed of the porcupine's tail embedded quills into the dog's face and mouth. A porcupine was not easily provoked. Nor showed fear. This one began to explore his new freedom inside Stoney Creek school by lumbering between two rows of chairs.

Becky pierced my eardrums with a screech from behind me, then ran to the back corner of the room.

"How far can they shoot their quills?!" she wailed.

My amusement was fed by Mr. Penski's answer. "About 50 yards or so, Becky. You'd better back up!" Becky whimpered, with her fists clenched to her face, pressing further into the corner, if only the walls would give way. Other girls left their desks at the sound of the news and moved to the back of the room. Ernie went with them. The guffaws from the rest of us who had seen a porcupine in action filled the classroom until Mr. Penski settled everyone down but Becky. The porcupine had ventured halfway toward the back.

"Okay, Axel," Mr. Penski said, "put your pet back in the box."

That was easier said than done, I imagined, wondering how Axel got a porcupine into a toolbox in the first place. Axel searched the room, then settled on two dowels used to prop windows open on warm days. Axel chased the creature between desk legs like a stick-juggler with a prickly porcupine for a baton. It took the rest of science class for Axel to accomplish his crazy feat, just before we were released to lunch.

3

Unwelcome Intrusion

"Ever visited the Northern Michigan Asylum?" I asked MaryAnne as she bit into her bologna sandwich. Mouth full, she signaled a time out. I had sat down backward on the bench, elbows behind me on the table, opposing Becky and facing my friend. Kids everywhere were talking louder than their neighbors, making a constant din. MaryAnne swallowed hard and furrowed her brow.

"Asylum? Why would I visit an asylum?"

"Just thought you might know about the loony bin in Traverse City that's letting their inmates loose."

"Shoe Makinen! Just because I used to live there doesn't mean I have anything to do with that place!"

I grinned at Becky across the table with her straight black hair and turned-up nose. The edges of her mouth curled, evidencing a smile.

I addressed MaryAnne again, "So you *do* know it."

"I know *of* it, I don't *know* it," she shot back.

I narrowed on MaryAnne, compelling her to a better explanation.

"We went by it once, just to see how big it was," MaryAnne justified, then spoke to Becky. "It's like a mansion. I was a lot younger then—it seemed like a castle. I still remember people taunting me, 'you're from Traverse City.' They meant, 'you must be crazy.'" MaryAnne returned to my attention, "Don't start that with me, Shoes."

"An innocent question," I said, both palms in the air.

MaryAnne's spunk had emerged beyond her red hair—a bright warning sign for most, not to spark her ire. But getting a rise out of MaryAnne was sport for me. Exploring the unknown heights of how riled MaryAnne might rise, over an asylum halfway across the country, was a venture worth taking. Hands still raised in surrender I departed, with a smirk for Becky. She smiled at me until she caught the tight purse of MaryAnne's rosy lips, then Becky feigned a look of disdain at me too. I shrugged, fully satisfied.

MaryAnne changed a great deal in seventh grade. For one, her striking, bright-orange tresses had developed into a deep, determined red. MaryAnne was no longer the shapeless, skinny girl of last year either. She had developed curves in places like . . . like the other girls in seventh grade had. She also sounded like them. MaryAnne lost her lisp. Her funny way of talking connected with me since the first day we walked to school together. With its disappearance, I felt that I'd lost a piece of our friendship. Still, she called me Shoes. My nickname wasn't nickname enough for

MaryAnne, she had told me she liked Shoes better. So Shoes had become my label—just between us.

As I made my way to the exit, there, at the head of the last row of tables, sat Buffalo Alice. Her beady eyes traced me as I purposed to leave the room without incident, to eat my lunch outside where the air was fresh and the spring breeze filled my senses.

"Makinen!" Buffalo grunted. "Still flirting with Miss DuPree, are you?"

I dared glance her way as I passed. Up close, I could see why Buffalo's eyes were too small for her face. The heaviness of her brow and swollen cheeks pushing up from below caused a permanent squint, day or night. Short, wiry brown hair, pasted away from her face as if it was trying to leave the scene, assembled at the back of Buffalo's head in a terrible collision. And that black dot on her forehead . . . I could have said something, but I didn't. Instead I moved past, careful not to reveal a spinal flinch Buffalo Alice triggered in me at the sound of my name. Luckily, I escaped without harm.

Buffalo Alice was coming up on two years at the Koskela's. Surprising the couple boarded her that long. With her parents locked up until Buffalo would be an adult, and the fact that she was a resident of Stoney Creek before she became orphaned, probably earned her more grace than other ruffians the Koskelas fostered from far and wide. If that wasn't enough, the word at school was that Mr. and Mrs. Hawthorne had relinquished their parental rights to

Buffalo Alice, given they no longer had sway over her. Even before their arrest, Buffalo's mom didn't include her in the Fourth of July parade, looking like she didn't much care for their only child. The way I figured it, the Koskela's reward for the kindness they showed Buffalo Alice on the night of the shooting was to get stuck with her, and now they had no way out.

As I made my way outside with my lunch pail, I wondered who was worse off, Axel or Buffalo Alice. I was glad neither of them were my problem, and that both Axel and Buffalo would remain at arm's length as long as I was keen to avoid them.

Still, I was thankful to Axel for speeding the morning, which brought me closer to checking traps. As I exited the schoolyard, I noticed a stranger lingering at the opposite end of the building in a dark overcoat, as if waiting for someone. *Strange*, I thought, for the man not to be working at this hour.

I jogged all the way home, gulped down chicken soup and fresh bread, grabbed my pack, and headed out the door, Oscar leading the way. Oscar knew exactly where we were going; the route through town to the bridge at the South Branch, then upstream to my trap line. I found my first set untouched, encased under a thin sheet of clear ice. With a walking stick I picked up along the way, I broke the ice in a semicircle from the dam, as far as the stick would reach. Oscar sniffed the beaver slide leading downstream. I whistled him on toward the next dam upriver. The second trap was in the same condition, untouched. I considered pulling it and moving the trap upstream beyond my last set, but decided to give the spot one more day.

As I maneuvered along the third dam, I spied from a distance that the set was no longer pristine like the others, revealed by melted snow, dirty from a struggle, and ice that had been recently broken in a wide arc. I quickened my step. Clearly visible at the bottom of my anchor pole was the black form of a beaver, bigger than any I had caught before. I heaved the pole loose from the pond mud then dragged its tip dam-side until my hand reached the leathery tail of the beaver, caught by its front leg, broken off, and hanging on by a tendon. The animal was a blanket, to be sure, maybe even a super-blanket. I would know once it was skinned and stretched on the woodshed wall. My flannel shirt enveloped me in an intense heat, fed by the heavy beat of my pulse as I lugged the beaver down the dam and onto the stream's edge. I would leave it there until my return, as its weight was too much to bear on the remaining check of the line.

A blanket beaver—my new accomplishment—put a spring in my step to all of the remaining sets, which were empty like the first. The final set turned my elation to discouragement. Where the trap was to be, there was nothing but the stubs of dam sticks I'd built as a platform, in shallow water not yet re-frozen. Gone was the trap, the anchor pole, and the wire that bound it to the dam.

I had lost a trap only once before. It was my own fault, having set the anchor pole too shallow in a hard-bottomed pond. The beaver had torn half the dam apart before chewing the ground pole and hauling the whole set under the ice. Here, there was not a hint of struggle. On the dam a few feet away were two fresh, white sticks gnawed clean by a beaver's chisel teeth—a common sight. But the sticks were stuck in the dam, standing at an angle to one another in the form of an "X".

The sight made my heart race. Large boot imprints had been left in the remaining snow on the dam, leading to the other side of the stream. Snuffy. There was no question in my mind. Snuffy believed this to be his land and thought he owned the South Branch, too. Oscar's hair stood up on his back as he inspected each imprint with his wet nose. I looked in every direction, scanning the woods, making sure I wasn't being watched. My alarm soon turned to resolve. Snuffy would not deter my success. He did not have claim on the land, the stream, or the beaver in it. Confident that I was alone, I determined to recover my losses by moving my line further upstream—tomorrow, after I had skinned, stretched, and measured the largest beaver I had ever laid hands on.

***

Exhausted from the heavy, dead weight on my back, I took a final break at the edge of Mrs. Krebbs' yard, dropping the load onto a small patch of snow. The return hike took longer than most, and the evening's darkness was upon me. Then it caught my eye again. There was no mistaking it this time—a light burned dimly inside the house where no light should be. Strange that I hadn't witnessed anyone around the place before, coming or going. The backyard's remnant of snow showed no signs of foot traffic. The front yard, exposed to spring sunshine, no longer sported snow. I trained my eye on the steady, dim glow, but could not identify movement inside. Yet I was certain this time that there was light.

4

Ghosts Alive!

At lunch the following day, MaryAnne took up her usual spot across from Becky. Uncomfortably close to Becky sat Buffalo Alice. I needed to tell MaryAnne about the light at Mrs. Krebbs' house. If anyone had an opinion about ghosts, it would be MaryAnne. It was part of the mystery that she was; not just that she had opinions, but that she had opinions that sprang out of a deep root, making her quite convincing, even if I didn't agree. When MaryAnne took up a topic she was sure about—though she sounded like a Bible freak to anyone within earshot—she never backed down. I needed to muster some of that fortitude for myself. And I would need it, with Buffalo abutting Becky at the lunch table, keeping guard over MaryAnne.

I had a seat to fake eating at the table with Mark for a few minutes, long enough to assess the risk. Mark's friendship to me was more a matter of convenience than real friends. He and I hunted squirrels, and trapped weasels in the winter, but beyond that, we did little together. Mark's work was on the farm, not on a trap line, no matter how great the reward.

Having set up my observation post, I spotted MaryAnne and Becky chatting about something out of earshot, MaryAnne carrying the conversation, as expected. She looked at Becky and then at Buffalo Alice. Becky leaned ever-so-slightly away from Buffalo Alice, subtle, but enough to be noticed. The sight looked as if frail Becky was attempting to balance the load from Buffalo's side of the bench.

"What are you smirking at, Shoe?" interjected Mark.

Snapping out of my gaze, I said, "Nothing. Well . . . take a look over there, at Becky's posture." Mark chawed a bite of overripe apple, then caught my line of sight, raising an eyebrow of delight. "Do you suppose she's sitting on the edge of her books, or does Buffalo smell that bad?" I asked.

Mark spat bits of apple across the table to nobody on the other side, choking back laughter. "Makinen!" Mark coughed, swallowing another laugh. "I don't think it's the books." We both reveled in knee-slapping laughter until Mark caught his breath again.

"What are you going to do about it?" he said.

"About what?"

"Buffalo Alice. She's guarding your girl—you know you want to talk to her, but you can't face the Buffalo."

"She's not my girl. MaryAnne is a friend—you know that, Mark. It's not that I *want* to talk to her, it's just that I have to tell her something before lunch ends."

"O-o-h, that urgent, huh? Too bad. You'll have to face the beast, and you can't do it, Shoe!"

With that, I picked up my bucket and marched straight to MaryAnne's table. Mark would not have the best of me, no matter the circumstance. Buffalo Alice's beady eyes tracked me all the way. I chose the bench seat next to MaryAnne, directly opposing Buffalo Alice, just to disprove Mark's point, though I dared not look straight ahead.

"Hi, MaryAnne. Becky." Becky smiled politely.

"Hi, Shoes," MaryAnne said, then leaned toward my ear and said in a quieter tone, "There's three of us here."

Elbow on the table, I cupped a hand to the side of my face, glared at MaryAnne, and gritted my teeth.

MaryAnne whispered, too loudly, "You said hi to Becky and me, but you forgot Alice."

Rolling my eyes to the back of my head and then forward again, I bore on MaryAnne once more, then turned to Buffalo Alice.

With scarcely breath enough to produce a sound I said, "Buh . . . Alice." The name didn't seem to fit. Buffalo sneered at me, open-mouthed, exposing teeth that pointed every direction on the compass. I retracted.

"MaryAnne, we've got to talk for a minute."

"Talking privately again?" Buffalo taunted.

"It'll just be a minute," I urged MaryAnne.

"Please excuse us," said MaryAnne to the other girls. We took our lunch and walked toward the door. Before we got outside, MaryAnne asked, with a hint of disappointment in her voice, "Why can't you be nice to Alice?"

I walked silently, looking for an answer or another question from MaryAnne. She always asked another question.

MaryAnne continued, "She's not like you and me— nobody is. But she's a human being, just like you and me, Shoes. She's made in the image of God."

Here we go, I thought. *Mrs. Krebbs oozing from MaryAnne*.

"That makes her an image-bearer. That's what I like to think. Why can't you be nice to her?"

No options. MaryAnne usually asked two or three questions, offering me an option. This time I faced the same, uneasy probe twice.

"She's mean."

MaryAnne stopped in the middle of the schoolyard to face me.

"She's mean and . . . and she's not nice-looking . . ."

MaryAnne steeled.

"Like you." The words, intended as a peace offering, hung in the air between us as MaryAnne's glare of accusation lingered. I squirmed in my skin, regretting that I hadn't something more brilliant to say.

"I mean . . . she's not as nice as—"

"Stop it, Shoes! I don't like what I'm hearing." MaryAnne paused for words. "I started praying for you after your grandma found the Treasure, and now I wonder—"

"So you think I need your prayers?" I retorted half-heartedly. MaryAnne possessed something I didn't. I'd known for a long time that MaryAnne saw things differently than me, there was just no telling how. I asked her once if blue was blue to her and not yellow. She thought I was crazy—just as crazy as she sounded to me—especially about liking Buffalo Alice and thinking that Buffalo looked like God.

"And now you wonder what?" I asked, looking for MaryAnne to finish her sentence.

"Nothing."

Nothing always meant something to MaryAnne. Leaning on past experience, I knew she wasn't going to let me in on it.

"So what did you want to talk to me about in private?"

"Nothin'," I said.

MaryAnne gave me the look that said she wouldn't settle for that answer.

"Just that I saw a light in Mrs. Krebbs' house."

"Are you sure? When?"

"When I came back from my trap line. I saw it twice, but there's nobody there. MaryAnne, what I really wanted to ask is, do you believe in ghosts?"

"No," MaryAnne responded with an inquisitive look. "I mean, there are angels, and there are evil spirits. The Bible talks all about that. But if you mean someone that came back from the dead, no. What are you saying, Shoes?"

"I don't know. At first it spooked me, thinking Mrs. Krebbs came back to live in her old house."

"It can't be Mrs. Krebbs," MaryAnne said with conviction. "There must be another explanation."

"Maybe. When I find out, you'll be the first to know."

My peace offering worked. MaryAnne half-smiled at me with both dimples firmly implanted in her rosy cheeks.

I grinned back. "Still friends?"

"Still friends." MaryAnne didn't sound convincing.

"What's the matter?"

"I want you to treat Alice as a friend too." MaryAnne gazed at the ground in front of her. Then almost to herself she said, "But I can't make you change that. Someone else is in charge of matters of the heart."

"A heart for Buffalo? Now seriously, MaryAnne."

"Still friends," she said, then turned on her heel toward the schoolhouse.

***

Large boot tracks, clear as mud in the front yard of Mrs. Krebbs house, confirmed to me that someone had been inside. Instead of racing home after school to rush out the door for my trap line, I detoured to the deceased woman's home to satisfy my curiosity about the glow that was sure to appear in the window again that night.

A clod of mud gripped the side of the stoop where someone had scraped their boot. I crouched low to inspect the evidence. *Not too long ago*, I surmised.

"Lookin' for somethin'?!"

Startled upright, I spun around and found myself face to face with a man I hadn't seen before. He was about a hand taller than me and wiry, from the little I could discern beneath his baggy clothes. The man wore work pants without holes and a shirt whose sleeves reached beyond his palms. Most striking was the black blazer that didn't appear to be his. Nobody wore a blazer in Stoney Creek except to church.

"Just checkin' the stoop," I stammered. "Mrs. Krebbs used to live here . . . and the house has been empty since she died. Was thinking someone else moved in." I glanced left, then right, considering my options in the event I needed a way of escape. Satisfied, I turned my attention back on the newcomer. What struck me then was the thinning hair on a guy I guessed to be in his thirties—light reddish, the wrong color for a man—and cropped to no more than half an inch, poking straight out everywhere like the quills on the tail of Axel's porcupine. The man grinned so wide his mouth stretched the lower half of his face horizontally, ending in a deep furrow on each cheek. An exposed single row of teeth had not been tended to for some time.

"Sounds like you know these parts," he slurred. The whites of his eyes popped as he stared straight through me. "Perhaps you can help me."

"Sure," I said, not wanting a confrontation. "What do you need?"

"I ain't got a lot of time. I come here to get me a girl, then I'll be gone—you follow?"

"Okay." I glanced again, wondering if it was my moment to bolt.

"What's your name, boy?"

"Shoe Makinen."

He thrust his bony hand at me. "The name's Gaspard. Gaspard Ruskin." His clammy, weak handshake added to my uneasiness. "I ain't been here long, got lots to do during the day, and found that there door open to lay my head at night. Can I trust ya, kid?"

I found myself nodding, only because I considered myself trustworthy, not that I wanted to be counted as his friend. The guy looked suspicious, and I doubted his story about Mrs. Krebbs' door being unlocked. It was true no one locked their doors in Stoney Creek, unless they were going to be gone for a while. And Mrs. Krebbs had been gone for more than a while.

"What'd you say your name was?"

"Shoe. Shoe Makinen."

"Strange . . . no matter. I'll just make this easy and call you Mac."

Strange was right. I hadn't seen a man so high-strung and prone to words. Gaspard stroked the scruff on his chin as his eyes raced to and fro across the muddy yard.

"Tell ya what. I'm in a bit of a fix. Like I said, I'm here to get a girl—I need someone to help me find her. You can do that fer me, don't ya think?"

I couldn't imagine why a grown man needed a boy my age to help him find a girl. It was clear to me this guy wasn't all there.

"I don't think I can help you find a girl," I said.

"Oh, but I bet you can. Why don't you come inside, uh?"

"I think I'll stay out here," I responded without hesitation as I began to back away to get away from the man. The last time I went in that house, someone died. I wasn't going back in, fearing this time it might be me.

"Now don't you be lookin' to run off." Gaspard sidestepped to discourage me from getting by. "Just you listen. You can help me, Mac. Last I heard, they took her to Stoney Creek, and this here is the only Stoney Creek in the state.

My blank stare must have written him a license to prattle on.

"The girl I'm lookin' fer is gotta be about yer age. She'd a come here a couple years back. Have you seen her?"

"What's her name?" I asked.

"Mildred." Gaspard's piercing gaze drifted from me to a group of chickadees flitting among the branches in the yard.

"We don't have any Mildreds in Stony Creek," I said. Gaspard smiled warily at the birds hopping from branch to branch in the warmth of spring.

"That was her birth name," he said. "Only name she shoulda got."

I caught my brow in a tight furrow, paining my face as I struggled to follow what the man was saying. My dismay didn't register with Gaspard as he continued his drivel.

"Her mama died same day she got born, and then I . . ." Gaspard's eyes darted around the yard as he rubbed the back of his neck. His face flushed. "They shouldn't have locked me up jus' fer takin' a few things. We needed 'em mor'n anyone. I only had the gun on me fer protection, ya know. Wasn't meaning to use it, but they weren't gonna listen." Gaspard's nostrils flared while he gathered his thoughts. "You know, them authorities tricked me into signin' her away."

I had heard enough. "I gotta get home," I said as I slipped toward the side of the house, where I could make a break for the backyard. Gaspard followed, moving in rhythm with me. Stepping backward, I continued, "If I don't get to my trap line, it'll be dark before I make it home." Gaspard's wild eyes transfixed on me as my hand reached the cold siding of the house, behind. Slowly, I slid along the damp, rough-painted boards until my fingers rounded the corner leading to the backyard. After a brief pause I spun, then lunged three long steps before Gaspard's words struck me in the back as if a hunter's arrow had pierced my lungs.

"She had red hair."

5

Shocking Revelation

The only redheads in Stoney Creek were Stinson's golden retriever and MaryAnne. The mere thought tormented me as I raced away. Was Gaspard really talking about MaryAnne—came here a couple years back, about my age? Red hair. How could he have known she had red hair unless what he said was true—that Gaspard saw her as a baby? My mind whirled, straining for a grasp on what I had heard. I halted in the brush behind the Standard station to gather my thoughts. Who was this guy? More wild-eyed than Lawrence Blankenshine. At least Lawrence kept to himself, talking to trees when he got social. But Gaspard— even his name was queer. Certainly not the introvert that Lawrence was—quite the opposite, in fact, prattling on as if *I* was his confidant. The guy was nuts.

That concept interrupted my thoughts. I had never considered *Lawrence* a candidate for an asylum, but Gaspard alarmed me. A case for the loony bin if I'd ever met one.

My brow must have lifted my entire face. Northern Michigan Asylum. It was all coming together, flooding over me far too rapidly. And did I hear him right? Mildred? Her birth name was Mildred?—"the only name she should have got," he said. And Gaspard ran at the mouth about being incarcerated, and now was looking for his . . . *his* girl.

MaryAnne DuPree was Gaspard's daughter!? Impossible!

Without further thought, I meandered the wrong way down the alley, away from home and toward the DuPree's. My mind was so fogged with the events of the past few minutes that my trap line had become of no interest. Instead, I wanted to find out the truth—straight from the horse's mouth. If what Gaspard said was factual, why hadn't MaryAnne told me? I was her only *real* confidant. So I thought.

Did MaryAnne have a past that she had been hiding from me? After all we'd been through? The millpond incident, Isaac's treasure, our brush with death over Snuffy's land.

My meandering sped to a brisk walk as I breathed deeply. Turning the corner at the end of the alley, I spied MaryAnne, late on her way home from school. Wanting to catch her before she approached her home, I whistled with the same, shrill pitch I used on Oscar. She didn't flinch. The thought struck me that MaryAnne wasn't Stinson's golden retriever. I broke into a dead run, intent on speaking to her alone.

"MaryAnne!" I yelled. She stopped and turned around, books hugged to her chest. When I reached her, I rested my hands on my knees, gasping for air.

"What's the matter, Shoes?"

"There's something you need to know," I said between breaths. MaryAnne tightened a smile.

"Change your mind about Alice?" she asked.

I shook my head emphatically. "It's not about Alice." My chest pounded as if I had run a mile. "It's about the ghost."

"Ghost? Shoes, we already talked about that. There's no such thing."

"Except when it's alive," I said.

"Shoes, what are you talking about?"

Having caught my breath, I surveyed MaryAnne as if seeing her for the very first time. She faced me, one toe of her riding boots pointed slightly inward. Dainty footwear for a girl her age. Given MaryAnne's spunk, it was remarkable that she carried it on such a small frame. The white lace hem of her skirt just above her boot hinted at the unique, feminine creature that she was. Delicate in ways that I had witnessed before, yet strong, and confident in her role. Her pale-green skirt suited the season and gathered at a wide band on a remarkably narrow waist, partly hidden by a yellow blouse and jaunty Polaire overcoat, open to the spring warmth—fashionable for Stoney Creek with its buckled cuffs and waistline. MaryAnne sported a tight smirk, adorned with the same dimples that had captivated me the first day I walked her to school. It was an accident, really, attending her to school. Still, we walked together, all the same. And the hair. Red hair—frequently braided French, as it was even now.

MaryAnne raised her brow as my gaze held too long.

The Miss DuPree I knew nurtured my intrigue, even beyond what eyes could discern. She produced a wonderment borne out in compassion inexplicable, a quiet strength I hadn't known in anyone else. Somehow, I hoped nothing would change, weighing the possibility that something already had.

"I have a question for you—" I started tentatively. "Before I tell you about the ghost."

MaryAnne cocked her head.

"Is there something you're not telling me?" I asked with the least accusation I could affect.

Her eyes narrowed while her dimples disappeared at the pursing of her lips.

"You can tell me, MaryAnne."

"I don't know what you're talking about," MaryAnne said. I fixed on her. She took up denial, shaking her head as her eyes darted toward home.

"I thought we were friends," I said. "I thought I was your close friend, a confidant."

"You *know* we're friends," MaryAnne retorted. "Can't you just speak English, Shoes? Stop beating around the bush and tell me what's going on."

"Fine. Since you won't fess up, I'll just lay it out there. MaryAnne is not your real name, is it?!"

"Shoe Makinen! Sometimes you get really weird on me. Of course it is!"

"But you had a different name once."

MaryAnne pulled her deep auburn brows together, then stopped hugging her books to hold them at her side. "What on God's green earth are you talking about?"

"Mildred," I said.

"Mildred?"

"That was your name, wasn't it? How come you've been hiding from me who you really are? You had a different father, a different mother, a different home, even a different name! I trusted you, MaryAnne. Now I wonder if the girl that messed up fifth grade has been messing with me all along." I filled my chest with one long breath. "Who are you, MaryAnne!?" I yelled.

MaryAnne fluttered her eyes, holding back tears that threatened to fall. She lifted her books again for one long moment, then thrust them into my chest before they fell to the dirt.

"How dare you!?" she cried. "You think I'm a fake?!" The tears that welled up in her eyes could be contained no more. One rolled down her left cheek, soon followed by the right. "How is it that you can be my friend, then the next minute, think that I would lie to your face—accuse me of being someone I'm not!? Where do you get these crazy ideas!?" MaryAnne's shoulders dropped. Her eyes streamed tears as fast as I'd seen tears roll. I wondered how she could see anything as we stood at the roadside in the afternoon sun.

Had I exposed her or had I betrayed her? Uncertainty supplanted confusion. I didn't know what more to say as I stood still as a frightened cat, contemplating what I had done. Could I have been wrong and damaged her trust in me? Or worse, what if I was right?

MaryAnne covered her eyes with the sleeve of her coat and stumbled toward home. I picked up her books, dusted the covers of her arithmetic and reader, and then followed. I didn't like the sounds of her sobbing. I had heard her cries before, whimpers of girlish fear, tears of joy for Grandma, but I hadn't endured such cries of pain. Her sobbing seared me, as I had been the one to inflict this on her. Carrying her books was the only gesture that seemed to fit. Suddenly, MaryAnne spun around. Her eyes, glassy red, probed me.

"Do you care to explain yourself?" MaryAnne said.

No words came. How could they? Just a moment ago I was on the defense, and how quickly MaryAnne turned it back on me. I hadn't done anything wrong—only wanted to know the truth about my friend. My hesitancy to answer only served to fuel the storm brewing inside MaryAnne.

"Talk to me!" she yelled.

I began gently, "The ghost in Mrs. Krebbs' house is a man from out of town, sleeping there at night. I think he's looking for you."

MaryAnne shook her head almost imperceptibly as she wiped away a continuous stream of tears.

"Let's get off the road," I said, motioning to the plum trees teeming with buds about to burst. I lightly touched the back of her coat, the wool like flames on my fingertips. Her soft braid brushed my wrist, electrifying all my senses. I dropped my hand, able to bear the sensation for only a moment.

Under the plums, and still overheated from my encounter with Gaspard, I took off my coat, spread it at the base of a tree and motioned MaryAnne to sit down. I flopped onto last year's weeds so MaryAnne could see me as I spoke. Her pained face focused on mine, expectantly.

I began again, careful not to extract more of her tears. "I stopped at Mrs. Krebbs' house on the way home to see if I could find any evidence of someone living there. As I was checking some tracks in the mud, a man came up behind me, wanting to know what I was doing. His name is Gaspard." MaryAnne's tears abated. She stared at me warily. I continued, for the first time realizing that what I was about to say might alarm her in ways I couldn't comprehend.

"The guy said he was looking for a girl and wanted me to help him. I was thinkin' he was trying to find a sweetheart, so I was fixin' to get outta there. But then he told me that she was about my age, came here a couple years ago, and before I left, he said, 'she has red hair.' That can only be you, MaryAnne."

"Why would someone be looking for me?"

I paused, not certain how to proceed. Part of me didn't want to experience any more of MaryAnne's hurt. Yet I wanted to protect her from the creep who claimed to be her dad.

"He says he's your birth father."

MaryAnne's mouth fell agape.

"He rambled on about your mother dying right after you were born and that he was put in jail for robbery. The guy is crazy—he got loose from the Northern Michigan Asylum, that's what I think. MaryAnne, he sounded like he knew who you were, that you were born with red hair, and that he signed over his rights to you, as your father, when he was in jail."

MaryAnne, as stiff as death, fixed on me with a mixture of astonishment and fear.

"Gaspard told me your real name is Mildred."

MaryAnne mouthed the name without a sound.

"There's something else you have to know," I said. "The creep said that once he gets his girl, he's going to be gone. He wants to take you away, MaryAnne."

Presently, MaryAnne began to shake her head slowly, then emphatically.

"No!" she snapped. "It can't be true. I won't believe it, Shoes. You must have heard him wrong. I'm not going to believe anything you're saying." MaryAnne stood up on my coat. "Give me my books. I'm going home."

I dropped my eyes from her small, resilient frame. Still sitting on the damp ground, I handed her the books, and she was gone.

6

Betrayed

I laid awake that night watching stars flicker through my bedroom window as Ricky snored. Bare tree branches glistened by the moonlight, nearly full. I thought about my traps, gone unchecked, about having to rise early to run the line before school. Contemplating trapping was a restful diversion from what truly occupied my mind.

I could have blamed it on Ricky's snoring, but my loss of sleep was because MaryAnne took me as a liar. Got me to thinking how she took it when I accused her of being a fake. I didn't want MaryAnne to think me a liar. What I said was true—so I thought. Her reaction, though, had me guessing. Did I hear what I thought I heard, or had I conjured some of it up at the surprise of being approached by a stranger living in Mrs. Krebbs' house? The events of the day played over in my mind—searching the yard, meeting the stranger, every word he spoke. I tried to piece it all together again as precisely as my memory allowed.

Revisiting that handshake gave me shivers as I laid under the warm covers of my bed. Gaspard, he said.

Gaspard . . . as hard as I tried, my weary mind could not recall his last name. Gaspard was enough to describe the creepy man in the black overcoat. It had been real, every bit of it. And I hadn't fabricated a tall tale for MaryAnne. She would have to come to believe me. Having replayed the scene more times than I could recall, the piece that prevented my sleep late into the night was Gaspard's words, "*I come here to get me a girl, then I'll be gone.*" At the time, it didn't register, but the more I played it over in my mind, the more I regretted not telling Dad.

I said not a word about the incident over dinner. Something told me I should have, but the altercation with MaryAnne gave me a heavy stomach and fuzzy thoughts. I had gone to bed early, complaining that I didn't feel good. I told Mom that was the reason why I didn't check my traps, and that I would have to get up early to check them in the morning. I hated that, the lying. Being around MaryAnne caused me to hate it all the more. I never once caught her in a lie, not even shading the truth. I was sure I would like myself better if she would only shade the truth a time or two. Yet her pure words magnetized me to her, causing me to see myself for what I was, so I remained careful not to tell a lie around her. But this was different—the events of the day justified not telling Dad and Mom. MaryAnne didn't need Mom calling on Mrs. DuPree to validate the news and raise an alarm.

***

A thunk outside of our house awakened me out of a deep sleep. How long I had slept, I couldn't tell. I sat up in bed to survey the dimly lit room. The moon's fading light entered in the casement window to cast long shadows across Ricky's covers. His snoring had ceased. What remained was heavy breathing from his bed on the opposite wall—the only sound in the room. Perhaps I had been dreaming.

Plink!

Startled, I rose to see what had struck the window. I pressed my nose to the glass and was alarmed by the distinct form of MaryAnne in the front yard, waving frantically with one hand, holding something at her side with the other. I blinked hard, unwilling to believe my eyes. It became clear that she saw my face at the window, as she beckoned me to come. I couldn't imagine what couldn't wait until morning. I heaved on the sash that was swelled with the moisture of spring and groaned from the strain. Ricky's breathing paused. He moaned, and then rolled over to face the wall. I waited until he began to breathe heavily again. Confident that he was asleep, I stuck my head out the window into the cold night air.

"What are you doing?" I said in a loud whisper.

"Come here." MaryAnne beckoned emphatically with her free hand.

I was awestruck. MaryAnne out for a walk at night was altogether out of character. I needed an immediate explanation. "Why are you out in the middle of the night?" I asked.

"Just come down here!" she demanded.

Afraid we might wake my parents, I closed the window and put on my school clothes. MaryAnne would not see me in pajamas, even if it was to be a brief interlude. I quietly navigated the stairs to the kitchen below. Oscar, startled by me in the entry, jumped to his feet, wagging his tail. I slipped on my coat and hat, then the two of us exited the back door. Oscar rounded the house first, yapping once at the form in the front yard. I hoped he didn't wake anyone. When I caught up, MaryAnne was petting Oscar, attempting to quell his excitement.

"MaryAnne, what are you doing?" I asked. In her hand was a carpet bag.

"I'm leaving."

"Leaving? For where?"

"I don't know yet."

I motioned MaryAnne toward the road in front of the house. "I don't want to wake my parents," I said. "How can you be leaving if you don't know where you're going?"

"They lied to me."

"Who lied?"

"Mom and Dad. The mom and dad that I *thought* were my mom and dad." MaryAnne's voice cracked. I stopped to face her since we were out of earshot of anyone still asleep.

"So Gaspard really is . . . you're saying you were . . . adopted?" The term felt like a swearword on my tongue.

MaryAnne nodded, choking back tears.

"They lied to me, Shoes. I'm not their daughter, and all this time they pretended that I was. They never told me the truth." MaryAnne's words halted between gasping sobs. "And that's not all of it!"

"What do you mean?" I asked.

"After I went home, I locked myself in my room. The things you told me—about being someone else—the idea wouldn't leave me alone. I kept thinking—what if it was true? When I came down for dinner, Mom and Dad were different, real quiet. Then Dad said, 'We have some news we wanted to share with you, MaryAnne.' I braced for the worst, my mind exploding with the idea that maybe I *wasn't* theirs. And then he told me. Dad said, 'MaryAnne, you're going to have a sister.'

"Your ma's . . . pregnant?!" I gasped.

MaryAnne pawed at her tears.

"It's what you always wanted," I continued, confused by MaryAnne's grief.

"It's not that," she cried. "My mom explained what they were talking about. She said, 'We've been praying about this for many months, honey, and God has given us peace about it.' I was so stunned, I couldn't comprehend right away what she was telling me. She said, 'How do I say this—you know that Alice Hawthorne has been fostered by the Koskelas for a long time, and she needs a permanent home. So your daddy and I have decided to adopt her as our very own.'

"Buffalo Alice is going to be your sister?!"

MaryAnne nodded, choking back sobs. "Mom must have seen the shock on my face 'cause she asked, 'Aren't you happy, MaryAnne? What's the matter, honey?' That's when I broke down. I ran up to my room and shut the door."

"So you ran away without getting an answer from them?"

MaryAnne shook her head and sniffled. "They both came in. Mom sat on my bed. I know they wanted me to have a better attitude about Alice, but . . ." MaryAnne sobbed. "I didn't want to say it, but Mom insisted that I tell her what was upsetting me. 'Was I born to you?' is how I put it. Mom's face went white and Dad stiffened up like someone stuck a gun to his back. Being an undercover guy, I thought Dad would have taken it easily, that he could handle anything. He didn't say a word!"

MaryAnne's tears glistened in the faint orange light that signaled the coming dawn.

"I'm sorry," I said. Feeble, given the circumstance, but the only words that came to me. MaryAnne gushed forth all that compelled her to leave the only home she knew.

"They didn't answer me. Seeing how Mom reacted, I asked her again. Kind of yelled, now that I think about it. I said, 'Well, was I?!' Mom's eyes got watery, then she said, 'Well, honey, we were going to talk to you about that someday.' Someday?! Someday!!?" MaryAnne yelled loud enough to wake the neighborhood, I feared.

"I'm almost thirteen! How many more years were they going to lie to me, adopt somebody else, pretending like I was their daughter? No wonder Mom never talked about the day I was born."

MaryAnne dropped her bag, covered both eyes with the palms of her hands, then sobbed uncontrollably.

I don't know why I did it. She wasn't "my girl" like Mark said. Perhaps my response to MaryAnne was a substitute for having no words of comfort to give my friend. I pulled MaryAnne to me and wrapped her in my arms. She trembled in my embrace, the gentle warmth of her hair beneath my chin. MaryAnne's rigid shoulders sagged, and then her body melted into mine as she wept. I could have held her there until the following day.

7

Trapped

"**Y**ou're going to have to go back home, MaryAnne," I said softly. MaryAnne's sobs returned, her voice muffled as she spoke into my coat.

"Who am I, Shoes?"

I used to hate the fact that she called me Shoes. I saw it as an act of defiance on her part—that she wouldn't call me by my real nickname, Shoe. But in that moment, her name for me became truly special, a treasure between us that I hoped would never wane.

"You're MaryAnne," I said. She left my embrace, troubled.

"That's who I *was*," she said, "until last night. Now I'm supposed to have a sister that's nothing like me, my birth mom is dead, my parents, who I thought I could trust, are not my real parents, and my *real* dad sounds like a lunatic—who's trying to kidnap me! What else could go wrong?" MaryAnne half-yelled and blinked back more tears. "Don't you see, Shoes? I'm not the MaryAnne you thought I was."

"You're still my friend."

She stared through my chest. "I'm not the MaryAnne *I* thought I was."

The pain of her words made my stomach turn. I tried to imagine the ache MaryAnne suffered inside.

"Is he really that bad?" she asked.

"Who?"

"My birth father—Gaspard, you said his name was, right?"

"Huh, MaryAnne!" I recoiled at the thought as I raised my brow and let my mouth fall agape. A ray of hope on MaryAnne's face dashed in disappointment as she bit her top lip.

"Alice was right. I don't belong here," she said.

"Alice told you that?"

"Don't you remember? The time you put pencils in my hair and I didn't know it? That's when Mrs. LeMarche called me up front to pass out papers and your pencil flew out of my braid and stuck Alice in the forehead." I grinned at the recollection. The beginnings of a smile curled MaryAnne's lips as she waved her head back and forth.

"She still has a black dot there from my pencil lead," I snickered. MaryAnne broke into a smile.

"You belong here, MaryAnne," I said. "You need to go back home before your mom and dad find out that you're not in bed."

"I can't," she replied with certainty, picking up her bag. MaryAnne blew steam into the crisp morning air.

"You have to," I said.

MaryAnne pursed her lips and shook her head. "You don't understand, Shoes. How can I go back there—where I've been lied to my whole life? I wonder what God's been doing with me—is this some kind of cruel joke of his?"

"Don't talk like that," I interrupted. MaryAnne was the one person I trusted about the things of God, besides the pastor, but I didn't talk to him much except for "good morning" on Sundays. MaryAnne's faith in God, though odd, was a shelter of stability for me after all that had shaken Stoney Creek in the last two years. I didn't like the sound of her lashing out at the One she put her trust in.

"Why *shouldn't* I ask?" MaryAnne said. "I wonder if he cares for me at all."

I searched for something to say to the one friend I cared about the most. "You're a . . . what do you call it? You're an image-bearer, MaryAnne. That's what you said about Buffalo Alice. You called Ricky that too. If *they* can bear God's image, then you, of all people, still bear his image too." The words surprised me. I was desperate, looking for some way to stop MaryAnne's absurd decision to run off. She paused with an air of contemplation.

"I'll tell you what," I said. "Since you don't know where to go, and I've got to check my traps before school, why don't you come with me? We can figure it out together—time enough for you to make a plan. What do you say?" MaryAnne nodded. "Wait here while I grab my pack."

A perfect diversion, I thought. I couldn't let MaryAnne just run away. This was no time for good-bye. I contemplated telling someone, to get help, but to wake Mom and Dad would be a betrayal of my friend. I was sure I could talk sense into her in the couple of hours it would take for us to run my trap line together. Mom knew I was to be out early. She wouldn't miss me, and we'd be back in time for school as if nothing had happened.

I found my pack in the woodshed where I'd left it. I made sure that my hatchet, pliers, and skinning knife were still inside—everything I needed to make a reset. Oscar followed me as I ran back to the front road. *Good*, I sighed to myself. MaryAnne was still there.

"Come on," I said.

I had pack in hand, and Oscar instinctively knew what we were doing. He led the way through the alley, out of town, down the road to the bridge over the South Branch.

"How far are we going?" MaryAnne asked when we were but halfway to the river, which was just the beginning of the trip.

"We'll be at my first trap in another ten minutes," I said. I looked over my shoulder at MaryAnne, trailing slightly behind. She wore the same clothes as yesterday, all dressed up and nowhere to go, except for a trapping expedition. I'd never had a girl trapping, I thought. *Good catch*, I teased myself.

"What are you smiling at?" asked MaryAnne.

"Nothing," I lied, glancing at her again. "Just glad to have a friend with me on my route." It would have been a comical sight if anyone could have seen it. The sun was just promising to rise as I strutted along the road with my beaver sack over one shoulder and a girl at my side in a pretty skirt, a jaunty overcoat, carpetbag in hand. I suppressed another grin.

***

My first trap was set just as it had been two days ago, iced over, undisturbed. MaryAnne watched as I pulled up the anchor pole.

"This one's going upstream," I told her with the most confident voice I could muster. "It's not doing any good here. Planned on moving one of these the other day—to a different plug up there that looks promising." I motioned upstream with a nod of my head and bold resolve.

"Oh," MaryAnne said with disinterest.

Dejected, I sprung the No. 4, double-spring steel trap with a slaying jab of my grounding stake. Designed to heighten MaryAnne's interest, a quick glance at her told me the demonstration was to no avail. I shoved the trap into my pack with its chain and wire, then picked up the anchor pole and grounding stake, expecting to use them on the next set.

"C'mon," I said. "If we hurry, we'll have time for a hot breakfast at my house."

"I'm not going home, if that's what you're thinking," said MaryAnne.

"Your choice," I said. "Either way, you need a plan."

"I know," she said, almost to herself.

My second set was a success—a good-sized beaver, caught by its webbed rear foot. Having pulled up the pole with the animal attached, I stepped on both steel springs, released the beaver's paw, then rolled the musky-smelling animal over on the dam to display my prize. Oscar gave the carcass a brief sniff, then followed his nose elsewhere. I pulled back the gums of the beaver to show off its long yellow teeth, one of them chipped, still sharp as a chisel. The width of its body and rubbery tail revealed the animal's strength and cleared up why the drowning wire was kinked every inch.

"This one put up quite a fight," I said, then sat down with my pliers to straighten every bend so the chain would easily slide down the wire for the next hapless beaver. MaryAnne gawked at the dead animal on the dam.

"That's disgusting," she said.

"Nine dollars, at least."

MaryAnne studied the icy pond. "What am I going to do, Shoes?" she asked wistfully, hands deep in her pockets, shoulders shivering.

I shrugged. "By the time we've made it all the way upstream where I'm going to set this last trap, we'll both be ready for a warm place. You'll figure it out by then." I wasn't sure she would, but I was banking on MaryAnne's tender, delicate side to win out in the end, hoping our trip would be long enough for her to come to her senses.

Oscar led us upstream, his nose tracking every step we'd made the previous time. My seventh and last set was undisturbed—no "X" formed with sticks on the dam. No new tracks, either. I breathed a sigh of relief, not wanting to explain Snuffy to MaryAnne. She had enough to worry about at the moment. I used the drowning pole to crack the thin ice on the surface of the pond surrounding the set, and then followed MaryAnne as we retraced our steps along the top of the dam.

Without a trail to follow upstream for setting the last of my traps, I led MaryAnne through patches of thick brush and around fallen trees, cut down by active beaver. I saw on MaryAnne's face that she had had about enough. My calculations were right, I surmised, that she would be ready for a warm, familiar place before we turned around. I would let *her* bring it up, though. No sense in me rubbing it in.

Crows cawed overhead, a welcome sign of spring. Before long, I heard the familiar sound of water rushing through the sticks of a beaver dam, still not in sight.

"Just a little further," I said as I waited for MaryAnne, who wrestled her carpetbag from a stand of tag alders.

"Ah-h-h," she exclaimed in frustration. "Are we going to turn back soon?"

A grin crossed my face, but I was careful not to let her see it.

"Only a few more minutes," I said. "C'mon, we'll be done before you know it."

The final dam, not as old as the others, spilled over with icy water at several points along its length. I advised MaryAnne to stay ashore as I ventured to the middle to locate where beaver would cross. Having found a well-used slide I set to work, driving stakes, smoothing wire, and building a makeshift pad for the trap to lie on just below the water's surface.

I glanced at MaryAnne as I worked. She angled against a large tamarack, arms folded, bag on the ground. Her look of impatience urged me to work faster, seeing how "turning back" had escaped her lips. I stepped precariously on both springs of the trap and bent over to splay open its steel jaws when suddenly MaryAnne let out a chilling scream that was cut dreadfully short. The trap snapped shut as I rose abruptly to a chilling sight.

MaryAnne stood ramrod straight, eyes wide, mouth agape, with the dusky barrel of a rifle in her back, held tight in Snuffy's grip.

8

Detained

"Get off the dam!" Snuffy yelled over the rush of water under my feet. Oscar barked viscously, teeth bared at Snuffy's heel. I hoisted my pack with the beaver inside and carefully made my way to the river's edge. As I stepped onto the bank, Snuffy drove the gun barrel hard against MaryAnne.

"Get the dog off me," Snuffy snarled, "before you regret it."

"Oscar!" Oscar backed away at my command. A low growl hung in the back of his throat as he paced in a half-circle just outside swinging distance.

With his eyes on me, Snuffy said, "Trespassin' again, are ya?"

I responded with a stoic gaze, knowing Snuffy had no claim over the forestry land he was on, nor the waters of the South Branch. That was made plain after our confrontation near the rock pile in Isaac's field. He was a squatter, illegally living in uninhabited wilderness. That fact didn't deter Snuffy, however. He was still as belligerent as that fateful rainy day when he'd brandished his gun at us the first time. The memory gave me shivers. His stocky jaunt, the wretched breath, the creepy look he gave MaryAnne when he reached out to stroke her hair—that last image of the hermit steadied my resolve against him.

"I see ya brought the pretty redhead with ya again," Snuffy sniggered.

I took a deep breath of cold air and locked eyes with MaryAnne. She mouthed a flurry of words with her eyes pinched shut. When she opened them again, the fear in her face cried for help as I posed helpless myself—without a plan.

"Git over there," Snuffy signaled with a dirty red hat precariously perched on the top of his head. The nod sent greasy strands of hair across his flushed face, bulbous nose and scruffy, red beard. He spat a strand of hair out of his mouth with a brown stream of chew juice. Not wanting MaryAnne hurt, I moved into the woods while he directed her to fall in behind me.

"Follow that path ahead a ya," Snuffy ordered. There was no path that I could make out, which prompted Snuffy to yell me back on course every few steps. We were marching upstream, beyond familiar territory, but closer, I knew, to Isaac's field and the land Snuffy called home. I kept a steady pace, not wanting more trouble than we'd already fallen into. Still, nothing hindered Snuffy's cantankerous ramblings.

"You good fer nothin' kids ain't much fer learnin' ere ya? 'Th'wise, you'd a kept far clear a here. Think yer takin' Clem Ruskin for a fool? Well, ya ain't gonna git away with it this time."

Hearing Snuffy's real name stopped me in my tracks. *Clem Ruskin*. With all my senses on red alert, the familiarity of the surname struck home. I turned around out of concern for MaryAnne. Her cheeks, tear-stained afresh, were as crimson as ever. She furrowed a helpless fear at me.

"Whatcha stoppin' fer?!" Snuffy yelled. "March on, young-un! We got ourselves some hoofing to do!"

Ruskin was the same last name Gaspard had used. I anguished at the thought. Clem Ruskin, Gaspard Ruskin— might MaryAnne be related to them both?

We tromped onward, giving me time to conjure up a plan. Trouble was, nothing particularly brilliant was coming to mind. Clem being Gaspard's relative fogged my thinking. I found myself thankful that I hadn't remembered Gaspard's last name for MaryAnne to have put the two together.

I guessed we had gone about half a mile when the weight of the dead beaver in my pack trained my thoughts on taking an assessment of our resources. First I looked to and fro, having not heard Oscar's growl for some time. He appeared to have gone, which struck me as odd. No dog. One resource amiss. There was MaryAnne's carpetbag, still in hand. No telling what she'd brought for the trip. Pliers in the upper right pocket of my sack, hatchet in the main opening with the beaver, a coil of 9-gauge wire, and my jackknife still in the lower left pocket. Not much of a defense against Snuffy's rifle, bringing up the rear of our small parade. Glancing behind, I spied the muzzle at MaryAnne's side—a relief that she no longer had to feel it at her back. She hadn't made a peep since her scream at the dam. I hoped she was doing all right, then I wondered if MaryAnne was still thinking of running away.

Our brush-infested trek upstream opened to a narrow trail, evidence that we were getting closer to Snuffy's home.

"Keep a move-on, girly," Snuffy said to MaryAnne, who had slowed after being on her feet since before dawn. The bright sunrise was upon us. Mom would be preparing breakfast about now, I imagined. Before long we came to a small, muddy clearing at the river's edge. Remnants of a white-tail buck hung on a pole lashed between two elms. Still hanging by its antlers, what remained were bones, sinew, and hide. *Poacher,* I thought. Then, what was to be expected of an obstinate, angry hermit? Beyond the deer stood an odd-shaped hut fashioned out of arched poles lashed together at the peak, covered with large pieces of bark forming walls and a roof. At the center of the dirty yard was a ring of stones, embers smoldering. Smoke combined with rotting flesh bathed the hermit's yard in a sickening stench. All around were implements of wood and stone, tools I supposed, rifle shell casings scattered about, a muddy piece of cloth, and the skeletal remains of a rodent—muskrat, I was sure, by the four long incisors protruding from a narrow skull, a sight I had seen repeatedly from having skinned more muskrats than I cared to remember. Snuffy stopped us near a small maple a few feet from the fire ring.

"Stay put!" he said as he searched his pockets for something. Satisfied, he pulled out a length of rope, held it in his teeth, then rifled through his pockets again. I took the opportunity to swing my pack to one shoulder. As I did, I heard the faint sound of two short whistle blasts from the sawmill—Dad would be leaving home for work soon.

"Did you hear that?" I asked emphatically, drawing Snuffy's attention elsewhere.

"What?!" he snapped.

"I think I heard the mill whistle from here."

"And what matters that to you, Makinen?!"

I shrugged. "Just thought I heard it, is all."

I was surprised that Snuffy remembered my name. Two appearances in "his" field must have seared me into his memory. Not the place I wanted to be.

Snuffy continued to search his pockets. "Now where in tarnation . . . ?"

In his frustration, Snuffy lost his focus on me and MaryAnne. I took the opportunity to slide my hand into the pack pocket that was sure to hold my knife, a slim jackknife I always carried trapping—for whittling, skinning . . . and cutting rope in a pinch. My heart leapt as my fingers gripped the cold metal. With the stealth of a seasoned hunter, I pushed the knife up the back of my hand until one end of it tucked under my shirt sleeve. Feigning an itchy eye, I raised my right hand to my face, allowing the knife to slip down my sleeve to the elbow. Then in a long stretch over my head, the cold steel of the knife slid past my elbow to nearly the pit of my arm, like a cube of ice. A cold chill never felt so good.

"Whatcha doin'?!" snapped Snuffy with angry suspicion.

"Just stretchin'," I said. "It's been a long walk."

Snuffy stared at me warily. Having found *his* knife, he cut the rope in two, handed one half to me and said, "Now tie her up!"

I cocked my head at him. Snuffy shoved the barrel of the gun to my chest.

"On the tree, stupid!" he snarled, then turned to MaryAnne. "Sit down, sweet thang, and put your hands behind your back."

Careful not to let my jackknife slip out, I pinched it under my arm, then kneeled behind MaryAnne. "Tell me if it hurts," I whispered.

"Better be tight, Makinen, or you'll pay for it!" snapped Snuffy.

I pulled the rope tight enough for Snuffy's inspection, but not so tight as to hurt MaryAnne.

"You okay?" I whispered.

MaryAnne sniffed and nodded her head. I knew she wasn't telling the truth. On the outside, she looked weary. On the inside, I loathed the thought. MaryAnne had suffered a tearing of the heart, the pain of which I couldn't know. Somehow, it was tearing me up inside too.

"Tell me it's going to get better," she whimpered as I finished the knot.

"I'm going to get us out of here," I whispered.

"I'll be praying for you," MaryAnne said softly.

"Get a move-on!" Snuffy shoved me with his knee before I could stand, causing me to stumble. "Over there!" he said with a nod of his grimy hair.

I understood that to mean one of the two trees connected by a pole from which the rotten deer hung. I dropped my pack and sat down at the base of one of the trees. Snuffy leaned his rifle against the other and turned around. My eyes followed a hole in the toe of one of his clod-hoppers as he retraced his steps. Then Snuffy pulled both of my arms back behind the tree, pinching the pocketknife between my bicep and the tree's trunk. *Perfect*, I thought, and then winced as he cinched the rope excruciatingly tight about my wrists.

9

Unhappy Greeting

"That should learn ya," Snuffy sneered, his breath burning my ear. "Now all that's left is figur'n' on what to do with the likes of the two of ya." Snuffy mumbled something else under his breath, picked up his rifle, then ambled to the door of his hut—if one could call it a door. The entrance to Snuffy's place was covered with a poor excuse, at best. At least the door MaryAnne and I cobbled together for my tree fort hung on two rusty hinges that groaned like a real entryway to a house. Not Snuffy's. His doorway was concealed with nothing more than the remnant of a rag rug, once carefully woven from colorful scraps of cloth, now stained a deep shade of grey, like the wood pole it hung from. Snuffy pushed the rug aside, still grumbling, then disappeared within.

I found myself glad that Snuffy tied both of us to face the fire ring, easily within his sight, glad that I had a knife on me, however impossible it was to put to use, and glad I could see MaryAnne. Strange, I thought, with nothing to do and no resources at hand, there were things to be glad about. Her profile—MaryAnne—pinned to a tree, bound as if in a straightjacket, set me to straining on the rope that cut deep into my wrists. Snuffy tied me so tight my circulation was cut short, lending little mobility to my fingers. The knife, still in my shirt, pressed tight against my arm, would do me no good, even if I managed to shake it loose. I wrenched on the cotton cords until I could bear the pain no more. I rested, pulled, then rested, making little progress.

"How are you, Shoes?" asked MaryAnne. I grimaced. It was just like MaryAnne to ask me how I was doing after I got her into this mess. Taking a girl trapping was risky enough; taking MaryAnne into Snuffy's territory was downright dumb. I knew that I would find myself in a heap of trouble from Dad if I ever got out of this predicament, enough to lose my trapping privileges for the rest of my teenage years, and trouble enough to be barred from MaryAnne's friendship. Mr. DuPree towed a hard line when it came to whom his daughter chummed with. I had a feeling my name would be so far down that list as to fall completely off once he discovered where his daughter was spending her free time. Losing my best friend would be a fate worse than detention in the stench of Snuffy's yard.

I strained on the rope again, driven to overcome any pain for MaryAnne. Fixing my eyes on her strengthened my resolve. MaryAnne, back straight against the trunk of the tree, head bowed, eyes clenched, moved her lips ever so slightly. Made me wonder how she thought her praying was going to get us untied.

"Any luck over there?" I interrupted. MaryAnne looked at me out of the corner of her eye without lifting her head, her fear curiously absent.

"To everything there is a season, Shoes," she said.

"What are you talking about?"

"A time to rend, and a time to sew, a time to keep silence, and a time to speak." MaryAnne closed her eyes and returned to her place of prayer.

If MaryAnne's real family tree wasn't mystery enough, there was the queer way in which she handled the worst of times. Praying at a moment like this seemed inconsequential, pointless. MaryAnne had ceded when there was a battle to be fought—to be won—and it was far from me to give in with my head down.

"MaryAnne! We've got to figure a plan!" I whisper-yelled, not willing for her to give up just yet.

"What's all the racket out here?!" Snuffy burst forth, nearly tearing the rug off its nails. "There'll be no talkin' tween the two a ya, ya hear?"

I returned Snuffy's glare. He moved his attention to MaryAnne, who gave a brief start before she returned to her prayer position, mouthing without a sound.

"I said, did ya hear me, missy!?" Snuffy bent down, his face uncomfortably close to MaryAnne's.

MaryAnne, suddenly transported back to our reality, said "Yes," so softly, I wanted to touch her shoulder and tell her it would be okay. Even if I could reach out, I wasn't sure I would have words of reassurance.

So far, any exertion I gave the bindings on my wrists only served to deliver me pain. The rope stretched slightly, if at all. My knife, pressed onto my inside bicep, sent a throbbing ache up the side of my neck. Try as I might, I could not free it. If only I could turn a few degrees, I was sure the tree's trunk was narrower that direction. Still, it was only a distant hope, and I was running out of ideas to make our escape.

"Good! Ya heard me! That means there ain't gonna be no more talkin', lessen I'm expectin' somethin' first!" Snuffy whooped, then chortled with disgusting delight, stumbling around the fire ring, sipping something from a flask he slipped out of his dirty coat that had been tossed to the ground. "You's a sweet thang, missy. I've half a mind to git rid a yer trappin' friend there and keep ya fer myself." Snuffy ambled over to MaryAnne, then reached out to touch her hair.

"Gaspard wouldn't like that!"

The words surprised even me. In a desperate attempt to steer Snuffy away from MaryAnne, the off-chance that Snuffy knew Gaspard was my only defense. Turned out it was the one defense that sent Snuffy into retreat. His eyes flamed as he spun on me.

"Gaspard! Gaspard who-o-o?" Snuffy exhaled in my space, flask still in hand, with his other hand on his hip. Waiting for my answer, he took another swig.

"The only Gaspard you know," I ventured.

With that, Snuffy choked on his drink, spewing snuff-tainted whiskey in my face. Then he seized the flask to his belly and slapped his knee with the other hand in a full-blown guffaw. Sure that I had misjudged Snuffy's knowledge of the other Ruskin, I patiently waited to find out what was so funny, blinking sting from my eyes and shaking putrid droplets from the tip of my nose. Snuffy's laughter eventually subsided until he could speak without spitting in my face.

"The only Gaspard I know is holed up in the state penitentiary, spendin' the rest of his years with nutcases just like him!" Snuffy slapped his knee in succession, gasping for air as he roared. Suddenly, he stopped to stare me down. "What makes you think this Gaspard a yours wouldn' approve a me touchin' the little lady?" he said with a toothless sneer.

"'Cause she ain't yours," I said in his own language. Snuffy glanced to MaryAnne, then back to me, breathing heavily, void of understanding.

"She's Gaspard's daughter."

Snuffy stood bolt-upright, his hairy white gut protruding over his belt, peering out from the bottom of his shirt, stretched taut just above a large cavern which, no doubt, housed a belly button.

"Gaspard's daughter . . . ya don't say!" Snuffy narrowed on MaryAnne, his brow furrowed while he contemplated. "We'll I'll be d——" Fixing to cuss, Snuffy cut himself short in the presence of MaryAnne.

"So, you's the one!" Snuffy crept toward MaryAnne as if he was encroaching on a fawn haplessly caught in the trapper's snare. MaryAnne recoiled as Snuffy drew nigh. She pressed the back of her head deeper into the maple, if it were at all possible. I struggled forward, nothing yielding. Snuffy presented his bulbous nose to MaryAnne, greasy strands of hair dangling dangerously nearby. She turned her head sideways and riveted on me with an appeal of sickening disgust.

"What's the matter, sweetheart?" Snuffy asked, attempting to lock on her, nose to nose. "Mildred Ruskin . . . say hello to your uncle Clem."

10

Captor Captive

The ache in my gut dulled the pain in my wrists momentarily. It wasn't my purpose to break the news to MaryAnne. Though it was an act of desperation, my reason for exposing another member of MaryAnne's distant family was no consolation for the renewed pain MaryAnne bore on her countenance. Her eyes, clenched once more, could not hold back tears borne from the re-tearing of a yet-fresh wound. I scarcely could bear to look upon her. She mouthed words again, which I desired to hear. Words for only her and God, I supposed.

Snuffy's fascination with MaryAnne was short-lived.

"And what makes you so all-knowin' 'bout my brother? Yer sweetheart here tell ya this?"

Seems it was my turn for Snuffy's wrath. I shook my head.

"Then where'd ya get it?"

I didn't answer. The pain deep within told me I had done enough hurt to MaryAnne to last her a lifetime, maybe two. I doubted she would speak to me again if we lived to tell about the nightmare we were living.

"Don't toy with me, ya good-fer-nothin' . . . where'd ya get it?"

I looked at MaryAnne. Nothing changed. Her tears streamed, her eyes clenched, and her words of prayer silently streamed forth.

Snuffy took one last swig from his empty bottle and thrust it at the smoldering embers. His whiskey had run out, and with it, Snuffy's patience. With the force of a hot-nailed stallion, Snuffy drove the toe of his boot into my ribs, turning my entire body on the tree. I gasped for air as a burning sensation filled my chest and as the tree's trunk agonized both arms.

"All's I wanna know is who told ya 'bout my brother!?"

I coughed. "Gaspard," I said. In that moment, jarred loose by my new position, the warm metal handle of my jackknife slid down my arm, out of my sleeve, and rested neatly in the palm of my right hand. The sensation alerted all my senses. Having nearly given up on shaking the knife loose, I had lost hope that it would present itself where I be able to wrap it with my fingertips. My gaze immediately went to MaryAnne, eyes still closed, no more silent words. I wondered what she had been praying. My heart palpitated. In the interest of keeping Snuffy occupied, I dispensed more about his brother for him to chew on. "Gaspard's at Stoney Creek looking for his daughter that he gave up years ago."

Snuffy's eyes bulged. "We-e-ll, h-i-ide-e-e ho!" He spun on his heel to make another turn around the fire pit. "Ol' big brother Gaspard flew the cuckoo's nest. And now he's migrated all the way ta Stoney Creek to jump claim on the girl that never shoulda been his in the first place! What's gonna happen next?"

I wondered.

"Well, I'll tell ya what's *not* gonna happen!" Snuffy said with certitude. "Gaspard's not gettin' a girl from me twice!" With that, Snuffy lit the wick on his own diatribe. "Gaspard Ruskin on the loose, eh? I've heard it all now! How is it that this 'ere good-fer-nothin' state can't keep ahold a them that's clearly a danger to society? Tell me that!" Snuffy paced to and fro in front of MaryAnne, then me, drooling from one side of his mouth, spitting when saliva was present of mind. "Some spessmins b'long in a 'sylum, if ya know what I mean."

It was vividly clear to me what Clem Ruskin meant. Snuffy halted at my feet like the exclamation point on the end of an angry sentence while I strained both sets of fingers to grasp the blade of my jackknife. I found the catch with a thumbnail twice, but was unsuccessful in prying the blade open far enough to stay. Once, it snapped shut loudly enough for Snuffy to hear it, if he hadn't been caught in his tirade. He lumbered back to MaryAnne.

"I never in my life thought I'd see the likes of you again. You know where you's from, sugar plum?"

MaryAnne cast an empty gaze at the ground while her head shook no.

"No!? What's the matter? Somebody been lyin' to ya all these years? How'd ya get so old without knowin' nothin'? Why, ya gotta be eleven? Twelve? Ain't ya never been told who ya *really* are, Mildred?"

MaryAnne looked like one of those fountains I saw in a picture book in the school library—a statue with water trickling from it. Rock-still, she posed, water streaming from both eyes. *Still, she has tears to shed*, I thought in a temporary stupor.

"I asked ya a question, Mildred. And, like I told ya b'fore, ya talk when I talk at ya. I'll ask it again—ain't ya never been told who ya *really* are?"

Snuffy's prodding jarred me loose from my daze.

"Leave her alone!" I yelled.

Snuffy spun. "Shesh your trap, sonny. Our family business ain't none a your business."

Perhaps, at that moment, he was right. My business was to open my knife, find a way to cut one piece of rope, and then get us out of there as fast as humanly possible. I tried again, thumb in the groove, pulling the edge slightly, when the point of the blade caught on the bark of the tree. I pressed the handle forward, then *thunk!*—the welcome sound of a jackknife blade seated in its handle. My pulse raced.

Suddenly, the mill whistle sounded faintly in the distance. *Too early*, I thought, *too early for the noon hour*.

One . . . two . . . three long blasts—Stoney Creek's alarm!—the signal used when a house caught fire, the alert to a town of a state of emergency. *They know we're missing.*

Snuffy's pause indicated he heard the whistle too, but he appeared oblivious to its message. Returning to MaryAnne, he placed his hands on his hips, jutted his gut, then addressed her with the fullness of a criminal's authority.

"Let me tell you, Missy Mildred, it's about time fer yer learnin'."

MaryAnne remained stone-faced, eyes to the ground. I focused on the knife's edge, centered between my wrists, and wiggled it back and forth, careful to hold the blade in a single position, able to apply the slightest pressure on the rope.

"Ya see, Blanche was *my* girl. Ain't never was Gaspin's. That's what I called 'im then, Gaspin. Gaspard was too good a name fer 'im, cause he couldn't be counted on. Speshly when it come to takin' people's things. Like I said, Blanche was *my* girl, and I planned on doing it right—marryin' her soon as school let out. Blanche wanted ta finish eighth grade an I was gentleman enough to let her." Snuffy kicked a stone at the river, then looked MaryAnne in the eye. "Your mama and me never got that far." Snuffy tightened his lips. "She found herself with child . . . and it wadn't mine! 'Gaspard,' she told me. 'It were Gaspard's,'—like I was supposed to be understandin'."

Snuffy kicked MaryAnne's foot. "That was you, little missy."

Snuffy's tirade served to drive the knife's edge deeper into the cords binding my hands, despite the numbing of my fingers and a searing pain in my side. He continued to expose MaryAnne's painful past.

"Yer mama got her due fer it. She ain't lived four hours after you were born. And I'da gave Gaspin what he had comin'—I'da tore him limb from limb if he hadn't hid himself out." Snuffy spat a long stream of brown juice to MaryAnne's side. "Ya see? Gaspin stole my girl, and he ain't gonna do it again." Snuffy assessed MaryAnne as if she was a horse he was about to purchase. "Yeah, yer a Ruskin all right, got the red head a hair to prove it," chuckled Snuffy. Then, with a certain anger in his voice, "But you shoulda been a *Clem* Ruskin child. You shoulda been mine!"

Frustrated that I wasn't able to feel any progress my knife was making, I wished I had sharpened it earlier, to a razor's edge. My only hope was to continue rubbing the same spot with as much force as my fingertips could provide.

MaryAnne hadn't looked at me since Snuffy began his rant, her gaze fixed on the dirt in front of her. Every now and then, her eyelids closed for a few moments while she shut out the horrid scene. I worried for her—for the first time, really. MaryAnne was always able to manage well enough on her own, a sturdy girl for her small frame. Now, when she desperately needed help, I was helpless myself. I wondered where she was when she closed her eyes—in the warmth of her own bed at home, with God in prayer, or simply suffering in silence in this wretched place? *Cut, knife cut*, I thought as I moved the blade steadily back and forth.

"Stay with me, Mildred," Snuffy said, coaxing MaryAnne's eyes open. "You're mine now." Snuffy's cavernous sneer of rotted teeth sickened me as he swooned on MaryAnne.

Suddenly, the rope yielded slightly, offering ample movement of my fingers.

Snuffy crouched low toward MaryAnne, teetering to keep his balance. "Come to Uncle, sweet thang."

The rope gave up its last thread. I scrambled to shake it loose from my hands, tugging at my aching arms, still wrapped around the tree.

Snuffy moved closer to MaryAnne, reaching forward with his tobacco-stained lips. She flung her head sideways, toward me.

My hands were free.

The hermit put one grubby hand on the tree trunk, then moved to face MaryAnne, blocking my view of her with the back of his nasty head.

In one swift motion I lunged forward, grabbed the top of my pack, and threw my entire strength into whirling a dead beaver overhead. With two long leaps the pack made its second loop as I trained my eye on the back of Snuffy's skull, which bobbed back and forth in an attempt to meet MaryAnne's face.

With deft precision the beaver's carcass, tucked nose-first into the pack, delivered a crippling blow to Snuffy's left ear, sending him to the muck. Snuffy rose to his knees, then stumbled on his feet in an effort to retreat before I struck him a second time in the shoulder, sending him to a patch of hard-pack gravel face-first. The sickening thud produced by his forehead striking the ground made me wince. Snuffy didn't move. He laid there, cheek firmly planted in the dirt, nose-to-nose with the long yellow-toothed muskrat skull, no longer lonely in the open yard of dirt. *Perfect pair*, I thought.

I retrieved my knife and cut MaryAnne loose.

"Are you okay?" I asked.

MaryAnne nodded. "Thank you, Shoes," she said as she rubbed her wrists.

"Hey, it was the least I could do."

"Can we go home now?"

"I thought you'd never ask," I said. "But there's something I need to finish first." Digging through my pack, I located my pliers and the coil of 9-gauge wire, which I crimped and broke in two. Then I wrestled both of Snuffy's fat arms to his back.

"Come here." I motioned to MaryAnne to help me hold the hermit's arms in place. She cringed.

"Disgusting," she said has she gingerly held his wrists, her pinkies in midair.

"More disgusting than a dead beaver?" I asked with a grin.

MaryAnne smiled. It must have been forever since I had seen those dimples.

"Good to see your smile again," I said.

I finished the wire by twisting it firmly, binding Snuffy's wrists to one another. I didn't need MaryAnne's assistance with the second loop of steel, which I cinched tightly about Snuffy's ankles. MaryAnne picked up her carpetbag, ready to go.

"There," I said. "Now when the muskrat comes to— looking for a companion—Snuffy won't have anywhere to move his kisser!"

MaryAnne raised her brow and shook her head as we rushed out of the yard.

11

Answered Prayer

Downriver was the only sure way home. Once the adrenalin that coursed through my veins began to subside, I became acutely aware that I was running out of air, each breath more shallow than the last, with a sharp dagger of pain deep inside my ribcage.

"I need to rest," I said.

We found a log near the river's edge, dropped our bags, and sat on damp, spongy wood. The place was peacefully quiet, where water flowed smoothly between the banks, no rushing sound of a beaver dam. Peaceful, too, was the knowledge that Snuffy was not in pursuit.

"You're hurting, aren't you," said MaryAnne.

I nodded. "I just need to catch my breath. It feels like a knife in my side every time I breathe."

"What can I do for you?"

"Nothing."

MaryAnne opened her bag and pulled out a peach-colored shawl—*one of her chosen items for running away*, I thought.

"Here," she said. "You probably have a broken rib. Can I wrap this around you to help the pain?"

"I guess."

"Let's get your jacket off." MaryAnne slipped my coat from my arms, then proceeded to wrap the shawl around my midsection. Her girl-scent tickled my nose in welcome contrast to the pungent stench of Snuffy's yard. MaryAnne snugged the shawl firmly, finishing with a knot in front, neatly decked with tassels that shimmered every time I exhaled.

"Nice," I said with a tinge of sarcasm.

MaryAnne grimaced.

"And thank you," I finished.

"You're welcome."

Her tender voice gave me pause. The day was but half over. MaryAnne had suffered the worst hours of her life, with every reason to cast blame on me, and yet my best friend drew from a reserve of kindness, so rare—something I'd seen in Mrs. Krebbs a time or two. MaryAnne's gesture of offering me her shawl sparked the memory of her mouthing words, eyes clenched while Snuffy ranted.

"So tell me," I said, "what were you praying back there?"

"Where?"

I tried to pinpoint a moment, when I realized that I'd caught MaryAnne in meditation throughout the entire morning.

"On the trail to Snuffy's yard . . . " I said, "when you were sitting against the tree . . . pick one."

MaryAnne contemplated, "I was praying for God's mercy when we were first caught. I see now that he protected us."

"Okay," I said as I struggled to put my coat back on. "What about when you were tied up, when Snuffy was taunting you?"

"I asked God if he would make a way of escape for us—he says he will, you know . . . and he did."

"Did he?" I asked, more to myself than to question MaryAnne's bedrock confidence.

"How did you get free?" she asked.

"I cut the rope with my knife."

"Why didn't you cut it sooner?"

"Am I on the witness stand?" I asked in defense. "I was doing my best. I slipped a knife in my sleeve before Snuffy tied us up, but it was pinched between my arm and the tree, and there was nothing I could do to shake it loose." Reliving the moment brought me back to that place. "That's when I noticed you mouthing something to God, wishing I could hear you."

MaryAnne interjected, "I kept asking God, please make a way for us to escape, no matter what it is."

I continued, "And then Snuffy kicked me so hard I spun partway around the tree." The thought sparked a sharp pain in my side again as I wrestled with my coat. I was unsuccessful at getting my other arm in, so MaryAnne pulled the sleeve forward within easy reach. "Thank you," I said, fighting back a feeling of helplessness. "Right after that is when the knife fell out."

"Sorry I wasn't more specific," said MaryAnne. "Maybe I could have saved you a broken rib." She smiled at me with her eyes.

I diverted my gaze, uncomfortable with where my heart was taking me, unsettled by the certainty with which MaryAnne spoke of God. Our circumstances *did* seem to be more than coincidence, yet to MaryAnne there *was* no coincidence, nothing to question, nothing but certain faith that God was with her, that God cared, that God answered her prayer. How I desired such fortitude! Being closer to MaryAnne was like being closer to God. I wasn't sure if I was ready for that. Besides, something more pressing was burning within me that I needed to get out of her.

"How are your wrists?" I asked, remembering the sight of harsh, red marks on her skin left by the rope.

MaryAnne looked at her wrist pensively, rubbing witness lines with her forefinger. "They're okay," she said.

It wasn't MaryAnne's wrists that I was chiefly concerned about. I knew they would heal without permanent scars, no lasting damage. I only asked about them as a precursor to what was haunting me from the moment I drove Snuffy's face into the turf. The question that burned like the searing pain in my ribs was a question regarding something that could not be reversed, an act of lasting consequence, the one question that needed answering the most.

"Did he kiss you?"

MaryAnne's eyes popped as her mouth fell agape.

"No! Thankfully, he did not! Y-y-yuck! That was s-o-o disgusting!" she exclaimed. "Are you trying to make me re-live it?!"

"No," I said with a deep sigh of relief. "I wanted to know that . . ."

MaryAnne's face was framed on me in disgust, jaw still wide, as if I somehow had abetted her misery.

"I just wanted to know that you've never been kissed," I said.

MaryAnne smiled, her inverted smile that told me everything was okay.

"Another answered prayer," she said.

12

Stunned

MaryAnne straggled behind, despite our slow pace. The weight of the beaver in my pack was painful on either shoulder. I took to lugging it by hand, but that felt no better. Had the beaver not been a fine catch, and the saving grace I needed to conquer Clem Ruskin, I might have left it in the woods to be retrieved another day. Our hike was turning out to be my longest journey home ever, while MaryAnne lollygagged behind.

"Are you coming?" I asked, stopping once more for her to catch up.

"I'm coming." MaryAnne said to the ground. The elation of freedom was now worn off; she appeared dejected.

"What's the matter?"

MaryAnne didn't respond as she approached, dropped her bag, then leaned against a raggy white birch and crossed her arms. I flopped onto my pack.

"I thought you were ready to go home."

"Me too. I guess I was ready to leave Snuffy." MaryAnne gazed into the woods, as if watching the remaining snow slowly melt in the warmth of the early afternoon. "Uncle Snuffy," she mumbled.

"Forget Snuffy!"

MaryAnne furrowed.

"Nothing has changed at home," I said. "Your dad and mom want you there. And they're probably searching everywhere for you—right now."

"I'm a Ruskin, Shoes. The kid of . . ." MaryAnne searched for a name. "Blanche—Blanche and Gaspard Ruskin . . ." MaryAnne continued, in her partial trance. "Snuffy's niece . . ."

"MaryAnne."

"Mildred."

"MaryAnne, stop it!"

"Stop what?" MaryAnne's focus turned on me. "Put yourself in my shoes . . . Shoes," she said sarcastically. "How would you feel right now if you were going home to a mom and dad that weren't your real parents—and never told you about it? What if Ricky wasn't your real brother? And what if Sophie wasn't your baby sister?"

I didn't know what to say. I *tried* to imagine with her, but the prospect was too far-fetched. "Shoes, think about it—what if *you* came from a family of half-wits?"

"That doesn't make you anything less than you are," I retorted.

MaryAnne's gaze fell back on nothing in particular. I got up, suppressed the pain, and hoisted my pack to one shoulder. MaryAnne didn't budge. I grabbed her wrist.

"We're going," I said.

She complied with heavy steps. It didn't occur to MaryAnne that she'd left her carpetbag for the squirrels, and I didn't bother to tell her.

***

The bridge was in sight when Oscar rushed upon us, his tail wagging frantically. I hadn't seen such an excited greeting since the last time we came home from Grandma's. I petted Oscar gingerly, holding him down, away from my side.

"Where you been, old boy?" With that, he ran back down the trail, up the bank, to the top of the bridge, where Dad stood, having caught sight of us.

"Shoe and MaryAnne! Where on earth have you been?" Dad punctuated the question by placing his hands on his hips. A moment later, he jogged down the bank in our direction—alarmed by our awkward pace, I presumed. I was still dragging MaryAnne by the wrist.

"What's the matter?" Dad asked, perceiving MaryAnne's bewilderment.

I dropped my pack. "We ran into Snuffy up there," I said.

Dad looked into MaryAnne's eyes. "Are you okay?"
MaryAnne snapped out of her stupor momentarily and
nodded.

"The whole town's been on the lookout for you two."
Dad turned his attention to me. "You look winded." Then
he tugged at the shawl tassels, drooping low out of my open
coat. "What's this?"

"I got kicked in the ribs. It's hard to breathe," I said, my
right hand across my chest.

Dad picked up my pack. "Think you can make it home
okay?"

I nodded.

"We should have the doc take a look."

Walking the gravel road was like free flight after
treading rough terrain by the river's edge. MaryAnne fell
behind again as I tried my best to keep up with Dad.

Dad was still agitated. "So tell me, why did you take
MaryAnne to check your traps? Adrien is fit to be tied—I
knew *you* would be gone before school, but neither of you
asked permission for MaryAnne. What were you thinking,
Shoe?"

"She was running away," I said, under my breath.

"What?"

I walked backwards momentarily to view my friend.
"You comin'?" I yelled. MaryAnne was keenly attentive to
her boots, moving at less than a girl's gait. "She's comin',"
I said to Dad.

"What's the matter, Shoe?" Dad asked quietly. "Did something bad happen back there?"

"It's a long story." I took a half-step to get close to Dad's ear. "She's adopted," I whispered.

Dad's eyes bulged. Then we both glanced back at MaryAnne, her head down, coat open in the spring breeze.

I knew Dad had many questions that needed answers, more than could be explained on our walk home—and within MaryAnne's earshot—so I filled Dad in on why I took her trapping with me, the setting of our last trap and our run-in with Snuffy—without opening the wound of the Ruskins in front of her. When I shared with Dad why Snuffy wasn't coming after us, Dad's brow reached for the sky. I took that as a compliment. We stopped again for MaryAnne to catch up.

"She doesn't want to go back home," I whispered aloud.

We trudged along, as fast as MaryAnne would allow, Dad lost in thought. Finally he said, "I'll get you two home and have a talk with Mr. DuPree, then I'll need to alert the mill to call off the search, and gather a posse for the Ruskins. Maybe MaryAnne will change her mind by then." Dad didn't sound hopeful. Nor was I.

***

Mom did a perfect demonstration of "worried sick" when we arrived—ashen, taut mouth, brow furrowed. I thought the sight of the two of us would have set her at ease.

"Shoe!" Mom scolded. "Oh, MaryAnne, where have you been?!" Mom whined as she embraced the girl. "Honey, we've all been so worried for you—for both of you," Mom recovered, looking my way.

I secretly rejoiced that it was MaryAnne who was honey and not me. Besides, a hug would have been excruciatingly painful, not to mention embarrassing.

"Let me tell you," Mom continued while she directed MaryAnne to sit at the kitchen table, "all of Stoney Creek has been on the hunt for you. When your mother checked your room this morning to find out why you weren't coming down for breakfast, why, she about had a breakdown when you were missing! How could you leave your mother like that and not tell her where you were going?"

Mom didn't expect an answer because she left no gaps between sentences for one of us to speak. Better that way than MaryAnne having to answer to Mom, I thought.

"I hope to God none of *my* children pull something like that on me; why, I'd be pushing up daisies, summer *or* winter. Poor Lillian, she couldn't bear to leave your father's side after she found him at the mill, but he had to join the search, and so, that dear woman nearly cried her sweet eyes out sitting in the very same chair you are in now, MaryAnne. What are you going to tell her?"

MaryAnne's empty gaze said it all, but Mom hadn't noticed.

"I hope you have a good explanation for your mama!"

Mom's tone shifted from gentle scolding to a full-blown tongue-lashing. "And, Shoe—to take a young lady *trapping*? Is *that* what you were doing with MaryAnne?" Mom answered her own question. "Well for Pete's sake, I hope that's *all* you were doing with her. There won't be a switch in that woodshed big enough for what you've got coming. You'd better hope there wasn't more going on between the two of you than—"

Mom had managed to fill every aching minute until Mr. and Mrs. DuPree busted through the back door.

"MaryAnne! Oh! MaryAnne!" Mrs. DuPree gushed as she scurried to plant a kiss on MaryAnne's cheek. "Are you okay, sweetheart?"

I hadn't witnessed a demeanor quite like MaryAnne's before, or since. Nothing in her countenance acknowledged the tender peck of her mother, nor the looming presence of her father.

"MaryAnne, honey, your mother is talking to you," Mr. DuPree said gently.

MaryAnne picked at her fingernail then fixed her eyes on the wall, straight ahead.

I didn't know who to hurt for most. Given the backdrop of Buffalo Alice, Gaspard, and Snuffy, I understood my friend's unspoken response. But the look on Mrs. DuPree's face caused me to draw a deep breath, then halt abruptly at the sharp catch in my ribs.

Mister looked regretfully at Missus as he pulled up a chair to one side of MaryAnne for his wife, and then flanked her with a seat for himself. I scooted backward, uncomfortably positioned at the head of the table.

"If you'll excuse me," Mom said, starting upstairs, "Sophie should be awake from her nap."

"Honey," said Mrs. DuPree, "if it's Alice you're concerned about, we can wait on that."

Mr. DuPree shook his head at his wife. "Arthur, could we have some time alone with MaryAnne, please?"

"Yes, sir," I said, straining to my feet.

"Daddy!" MaryAnne pleaded—her first word since I'd dragged my friend out of the woods. She cupped her hand to her dad's ear.

Mr. DuPree raised his brow. "All right," he said. "Shoe—Arthur . . . MaryAnne would like you to stay."

"Yes, sir." I caught MaryAnne's eye beholding mine. *This is how you can help,* she said, without uttering a word.

13

Full Disclosure

"Why did you run away?" asked Mr. DuPree.
Silence.

"Is it about Alice?"

More silence. The prospect of having Buffalo Alice as a sister was enough to make anyone run away, but there was a lot more to MaryAnne's flight from home, so much they didn't know. I locked on her to detect if she wanted me to say something, but she gave me no clue.

"You never told me that I was adopted," MaryAnne said to her hands.

"We're so sorry, honey," said her mother.

MaryAnne picked at her fingernail again. "Isn't that lying?"

Mr. DuPree looked up at his wife, then interjected, "MaryAnne . . . we thought we were protecting you. We wanted you to feel like our very own. The older you got, the more difficult it became to break the news to you." Mr.

DuPree's eyes darted across the kitchen. "Now we see how wrong that was."

"Will you forgive us?" The words came out in unison from her mom and dad. I squirmed.

MaryAnne said nothing.

Mrs. DuPree's tears fell when they could be contained no more. "I'm so sorry this had to come out with adopting Alice."

MaryAnne bit her top lip, shook her head, then looked at me. "You tell them, Shoes."

Mr. and Mrs. DuPree turned expectantly. I sat up from my slouch, not knowing where to start.

"Well . . . I can take the blame for getting us in trouble with Snuffy. When MaryAnne said she was running away, I tried to buy some time by taking her to check traps, since that was what I had to do anyway. I thought it might give her enough time to change her mind, and then go back home. Well, I guess it did, now that I think about it." I grinned mildly. Mister and Missus didn't recognize the whimsy.

I continued, "You see, I took one of my traps upstream—closer to Snuffy's stomping ground, and that's where he caught us, forced us to his hut and tied us up. I suppose the worst part of it was when Snuffy got in MaryAnne's face and said, 'Say hello to your uncle Clem.'"

MaryAnne shut her eyes and Mrs. DuPree clapped her hands over her mouth.

Mr. DuPree scowled. "He said what?"

"Snuffy is MaryAnne's uncle. I think that's what she's most upset about, sir—wouldn't you say, MaryAnne?"

MaryAnne clenched her eyes and pursed her lips.

"Wait a minute! How do you know?" said Mr. DuPree. "We thought the last name was a coincidence. Are you sure?" Mr. DuPree throttled. I reared in my seat, taken aback by how unnerved his speech had gotten.

"Oh, I think so. *Snuffy's* quite sure!" I said.

His mouth fell agape.

"I guess I was the one that started it all when I thought MaryAnne was lying to me about who she really was. You see, this guy—Gaspard—was looking for a girl about MaryAnne's age—"

Mr. DuPree slapped the table, eyes glued on me, and statued in the same position. I concluded that he was waiting for a better explanation.

"So, when the guy said that the girl he was looking for had red hair, I figured it must be MaryAnne. I had to find out, directly from her, if what the guy said was true. I was kind of mad that she never told me. That's when I caught up to MaryAnne going home from school and accused her of lying to me about who she really was."

Mr. DuPree sat on the edge of his chair, tightened his mouth, and then tucked his chin tight to his chest, "Gaspard?!"

"Uh-huh."

"Gaspard Ruskin?"

"Yes, sir," I said. "Do you know him?"

"Where did you see Gaspard Ruskin?!"

"At Mrs. Krebbs' house. He's been staying there nights and—"

Mr. DuPree stood abruptly, knocking his chair backward with a loud crash to the kitchen floor. It gave him no pause as he raced out of the house, slamming the screen door behind him, leaving the kitchen, and the rest of us, exposed to the cold March wind.

***

The doctor didn't waste much time on me.

"Looks like you've got more than one broken rib there, son." I might have told them that from the agony he applied by pushing onto every rib on my left side. The doctor didn't approve of MaryAnne's shawl and replaced it with two rolls of gauze and ample tape. Then he was off to something more pressing, leaving me in the care of Mom, who still fretted over MaryAnne and Mrs. DuPree.

"That Snuffy didn't touch you, did he?" Mom asked, with one hand on MaryAnne's shoulder.

"No," said MaryAnne.

"She got by unscathed, Mom." MaryAnne caught my eye. "Unblemished," I said with a grin.

My friend simpered—a welcome sight that soothed my pain.

Mrs. DuPree was unusually quiet, petting MaryAnne's hand while we waited for the men to return. Mom, however, was full of conjecture about what should happen with those two "hooligans."

"No telling what those two might have done if they had gotten away with it. Like I said, Lillian, we should pay attention to what's in the *Gazette*. My own family wouldn't listen about the asylum article, and here we are, quiet, little Stoney Creek, with one of those nut-cases prowling in our very own neighborhood!"

Mrs. DuPree stiffened, gawked at Mom, then rolled her eyes toward MaryAnne.

"Well," Mom floundered, visibly caught off guard that she was speaking of MaryAnne's birth father, "what I mean is that we should just be more aware of things."

Disconcerted voices outside silenced Mom. Mr. DuPree was heard talking rather loudly. Then Dad entered the house, followed by Sheriff Downing and Mr. DuPree. MaryAnne's dad dropped her carpetbag inconspicuously at the entryway.

The sheriff spoke first. "Hello, ladies." Sheriff Downing nodded to the moms. "Fancy meeting the two of you here again," he said to MaryAnne and me. "Seems like yesterday . . . except you're both a little bigger this time." Sheriff Downing chuckled, then facing awkward silence, he cleared his throat. "Clem Ruskin is in custody, thanks to you, Mr. Makinen. He'll be charged tomorrow." The sheriff coughed again and glanced at Mr. DuPree. "Now about this Gaspard fella. We can't find hide nor hair of him. I spoke with the director at the Northern Michigan Asylum. It seems he was an inmate there up until a few weeks ago; had a clean record, they say, so they let him go on good behavior—they've got nothing on him." The sheriff spoke as if settling a minor dispute. "Truth be told, even if this fella is in town, Gaspard Ruskin hasn't broken any law."

Mr. DuPree appealed, "But, Sheriff, what about stalking? Isn't there a law against that?"

"No, there isn't, Adrien. There's no law against *looking for* someone."

The tendons in Mr. DuPree's neck tightened. "He broke into the Krebbs house."

"Perhaps. It does appear that someone has been in the residence, but that's purely circumstantial at the moment."

Dad interjected, "Shoe, what can you tell the sheriff about Gaspard?"

"He's kinda queer."

"What do you mean by that, son?" asked the sheriff.

"His clothes were too big," I said, assembling my thoughts. "And he wore a suit jacket. He asked me to help him find a girl, which I thought was weird, and he talked a lot."

Sheriff raised his brow at me, then Dad and Mr. DuPree.

"No crime there."

Mr. DuPree clenched his jaw at the sheriff.

"We'll patrol the place when we get down this way," said the sheriff with an air of finality. "We're here to protect you folks, so if anything more comes of it, you call my office right away. Fair enough?"

"Thank you, Mr. Downing," said Dad as the sheriff exited.

"Would you look at the time!" worried Mom. "Supper won't fix itself." Mom rattled pots with enough force to break up a crowd.

Mr. DuPree glanced around the room uneasily. "Are you ready to go home, MaryAnne?"

MaryAnne rose from her chair. "Not yet."

Mom hushed a ringing pot cover with the palm of her hand at the sound of MaryAnne's resolute declaration. I stiffened. The room hung in suspense while I wondered where my friend got such audacity to address her parents without the slightest hint of disrespect. What was it that she drew on that gave MaryAnne the certitude to face a sorrowful mother, to stand unshakeable before her father, a man of great physical strength who towered over her small frame?

MaryAnne met her father's eye. "Not until I have a clear conscience," she said. "You asked if I'd forgive you," MaryAnne reflected, turning to her mother, "and I do. I forgive you both."

"Oh, sweetheart!" said her mother, jumping to her feet with youthful vim. She cradled MaryAnne's face in her hands and planted a lengthy kiss on her daughter's forehead. The DuPree family locked themselves in a three-way embrace, suspending us Makinens in uneasy wonderment. I paused to consider what that would be like. So tender was the moment that it prompted more rattling of dishes from Mom to splinter up the clan. Mom and Dad offered the DuPrees curt good-byes, my gaze escorted MaryAnne to the door, and then, too suddenly, they were gone.

14

Frontal Attack

My fear had been well founded. Dad saw to it that I pulled my traps the very next day, a Saturday. Yes, he said I did the right thing—after I found myself in the fix that I had gotten us into—but I was responsible for the predicament, and for bringing MaryAnne to a place she never should have been.

"Your trapping days are over," he said. "At least for the season."

As difficult as that was to swallow, I was grateful to have him with me on the line, seeing how I was in no condition to pull up stakes by myself. Our time together was spent in silence except when Dad had words of wisdom to impart to me.

As we navigated the first dam, "Shoe, it's better to stay out of a mess than to be a hero cleaning up the one you made."

"Yes, sir."

While wrestling one particularly difficult pole out of the mud, "You should have gotten help, rather than run off with MaryAnne."

"Yes, sir."

Yes, sir, was always the best answer with Dad—when I understood, and even when I did not. His final instruction, most unsettling, came to me as we turned down the alley toward home.

"Shoe, don't think you can fix what troubles MaryAnne."

"Yes, sir," I said reluctantly.

I *wanted* to help MaryAnne, to ease what troubled her. I knew I couldn't fix everything, but her troubles were practically mine—we'd discovered them together, lived and breathed the depths of her afflictions in tandem. MaryAnne might not have been my girl, but her troubles were assuredly my own.

***

Dad declared that the family would hang low for the weekend, out of touch with the townsfolk. I was to remain indoors after pulling my traps. We didn't even attend church on Sunday, to "let the boil settle down to a simmer," as Dad put it. It was just as well, as I didn't want to speak to anyone about it while I mended my ribs back to health. After being holed up for what seemed like a week, Monday arrived, a welcome spring day.

Released from confinement, my relief was short-lived when I discovered MaryAnne absent from class. School was never the same without my friend, and her absence the first day back from our misadventures filled me with much consternation. Had something gone wrong at home, things not resolved? Wasn't forgiveness supposed to be for keeps?

I anticipated MaryAnne and me facing the mob together. Instead, I was to go it alone, like a boxer pummeled in the fourth round, with misgivings about entering the ring and the lengthy stretch ahead. Ugly whisperings before class were clearly directed my way; the judgmental glances, the smirks. I settled into my desk at the opening bell. All I wanted was to navigate Monday without explanation, which is just how the day began until Mrs. Andersen left the room with Ernie to visit the school principal. Ernie had outgrown the corner and was now the one seventh-grader most familiar with the interior of the principal's office. They were gone but a moment when Mark turned in his chair and spoke at me with a voice for all to hear.

"Sounds like she's a *lot* more than a friend, Shoe."

I narrowed my eyes at him, surprised by Mark's combativeness.

"The only guy in history to take a girl out to his trap line on a first date!" Mark chortled jealously. Other guys laughed, Becky glared, and Buffalo Alice, two rows over, bore at me with a sneer of derision sharp enough to pierce bone.

Muscles between my shoulder blades tensed, pulling my fingers closed.

"Couldn't come up with a better plan than that to woo your girl?!" Mark jeered.

I slowly drew my right hand off the desk, fist clenched. I had never fought Mark. Fighting wasn't my thing. But Mark's round mug, lit with glee, begged for a smart correction.

"Leave him alone."

Mark stood while I spun in my chair at the sound of Axel Crossjaw.

"Well, look who found his voice," Mark said. "You have something to say about it?"

All laughter subsided as Mark awaited an answer.

"I said leave him alone." Axel had one hand on his desktop, the other near his satchel.

Mark, rebuked by a peer before his class—the lowest peer by teen standards—responded by leaving his own desk and approaching Axel, still seated. Axel paid no mind to Mark standing by his side. Instead, he spoke toward the empty seat in front of him.

"He took out Snuffy. More than a coward like you would ever dream of."

Tension filled the room, every eye trained on Mark as he deliberated his position before his peers. Dad's advice, still fresh, raced to the front and center of my consciousness, "Better to stay out of a mess than to be a hero cleaning up the one you made." Yes, sir, appeared to be the correct response, even for the scene playing out in full view of the entire class.

Mark lifted his hand slowly, then with his pinky, applied a tepid rap to the back of Axel's head, a strike so placid, perhaps because Mark would rather have avoided touching the guy's hair, that Axel's head scarcely moved. Mark's smirk was to be short-lived.

Had I blinked in that moment, I would have missed the speed of one agile motion as Axel rose from his chair and drove a lanky fist into Mark's sly grin. Desks crashed into one another in a chain-reaction pileup as Mark fell backward, unconstrained. Blood spewed from his nose and mouth almost instantaneously, splattered the floor, then pooled where Mark lay groaning.

Girls screamed in horror.

Axel sat down in his seat, relaxed, as if nothing happened. Then he pulled a paper from his satchel and hunched over the old remnant of schoolwork as if lost in study.

The classroom door flung open.

"What on earth is going on in here?!" exclaimed Mrs. Andersen.

Two students, caught in the fray, straightened their desks and sat back down. The rest of the class took studious positions, including me.

"The boys are fighting," one of the girls sobbed.

Axel hadn't looked up. Mark tottered to his feet, face in the crook of his arm to restrain blood that had already stained his khaki shirt a bright crimson.

"Who did this to you?" asked the teacher.

Mark glared at her without a word.

"Come with me, young man," she said. "I'm sure the principle will help you get to the bottom of this."

***

I was stunned to find Axel leaning against the sticky trunk of a spruce during lunch. Most certainly, he would have been expelled for fighting. Apparently Mark was still holding out. I approached Axel gingerly, catching his glance that told me he knew I was near.

"Thanks for that today," I said.

"Don't mention it," said Axel, eyes to the ground. I studied the spot in the dirt with him.

"Why did you do it?"

Axel shrugged. "Guys like Mark need to be put in their place."

I nodded, still not understanding Axel's motive in sticking up for me.

"Tell me how you took him out," he said.

"Excuse me?"

"Snuffy. Tell me how you did it."

I expected to have to replay the details that led up to Snuffy's demise, but never expected the question from

Axel. As I contemplated what to share, Dad's advice about not being a hero of your own mess weighed on me.

"I cut myself loose with a knife I hid in my sleeve," I said. "He wasn't looking, so I swung my pack at him. Had a beaver in it—a large one, I found out, after I stretched it. I swung it around twice," motioning my hands overhead, "as hard as I could toward the side of Snuffy's head."

Axel looked at me. A rare grin appeared on his face.

"I had to hit him twice to keep him down. Then I bound up his hands and feet with trapping wire and a good pair of pliers."

Axel's grin grew as he nodded idly.

"He wasn't going anywhere, I can tell you that," I concluded.

"It's been a long time comin'." Axel's sparse use of words left me hanging for more. Then he explained.

"Snuffy Ruskin's been poachin' our land as long as I can remember. Nothin' we done ever stopped 'im. Worst part of it was, he done it for the fun; thought it was a big game to take what was rightfully ours, callin' us trash, and a good bit of other choice words you don't wanna know."

"M-m-m," I said.

"You done 'im right."

I pushed my shoulders back at the only compliment ever known to be uttered by Axel Crossjaw. I hadn't imagined a feud had smoldered in the backwoods of Stoney Creek where land and trees went on forever, game a-plenty, enough hunting ground for all—and then some. Yet the

Crossjaws suffered at the hand of . . . MaryAnne's uncle. The connection jarred me once again.

"Thanks," Axel muttered.

"Don't mention it."

I found a tree of my own to lean on for lunch. Quiet was what I needed. Quiet and solitude. The third day since seeing MaryAnne. Were visions of Snuffy still lumbering through her head? What did she think of her new parents now, the only ones she'd ever known? Would MaryAnne rest, not having met her birth father, when he had been so close by? Where was she, anyway? I looked across the schoolyard in hopeful reaction to my own question. There, coming straight in my direction, was Buffalo Alice. I pretended not to see her, futile as it was, like Sophie does, covering her eyes to hide from the seeker.

"Makinen!" Buffalo Alice bellowed, her only address to me. "I have to apologize. I accused you of flirting with Miss DuPree the other day and I was wrong."

Buffalo's confession caught me off guard. I looked up from my sandwich just as she buried her hands in the layer over her hips.

"Flirting! A far cry from what you've got cookin' with MaryAnne! C'mon, tell me all about it. Nobody runs off in the woods with a girl without givin' me all the details!"

I addressed Buffalo Alice with a look of disgust.

"C'mon, Makinen. You can't hold out forever. Besides, I'll get it out of DuPree if you don't tell me first. It'd be better if you gave me your side of the story." Buffalo's shoulders rose as she drew in a deep breath of recovery from the traverse across the schoolyard. "Where is she, anyway? Did ya scare her off or somethin'?"

"Don't harass her," I said.

"What are you talkin' about? MaryAnne's my friend." Buffalo Alice's eyes narrowed to dark, puffy slits cut into an otherwise red face. "And you aren't going to tell me what to do!"

Becky and a couple others had inconspicuously wandered within earshot, but Buffalo's roar carried further beyond, drawing the attention of others. Keenly aware of another potentially explosive confrontation, I chose to diffuse it for the sake of MaryAnne.

"She's hurting right now."

"Why? What did you do to her?"

I caught myself grinding my teeth. "MaryAnne's going to need some time," I said. "Can you just leave her alone?!" Then, without awaiting an answer, I picked up my lunch bucket and headed for class.

15

Reunited

"Are you a good guy or a bad guy?" Ricky asked as I got ready for bed.

"What do you mean?"

Ricky pulled back his covers and sat up. "Some kids at school say you're a good guy 'cause you hit Snuffy. Other kids say you're a bad guy 'cause you ran away with MaryAnne. So, are you a good guy or a bad guy?"

I wanted to get in bed, sink into my pillow, and let the day's events fade off to sleep rather than become entangled in Ricky's nighttime web of conversation. Yet Ricky posed a question that begged an answer, a black-and-white, 7-year-old, make-it-simple-for-me answer. Thing was, the topic had developed far beyond simple to the inexplicably complex, especially for a first-grader.

"I don't know, Ricky."

Ricky's longing expectation wilted toward disappointment as I reconsidered what I should say. He looked up to me like I was some kind of hero. Not as lofty as Dad, but one of Ricky's heroes nonetheless.

"Most days I think I'm a good guy," I said through my t-shirt as I pulled it up over my head. "Then when I think I'm doing the right thing, folks think I'm the bad guy." I tossed my shirt at the wall below the windowsill. "Kind of like when you get in trouble and you think you didn't do anything wrong."

Ricky possessed a remarkable ability to wear his feelings on his baby face, which was telling me that his question had not been satisfied. I sat down on my bed.

"I *want* to be a good guy, Ricky. I don't always know *how*." I pulled the blankets up and rolled over, longing for a peaceful rest. The rustling of Ricky's covers told me that he was settling down to sleep himself.

"I want to be a good guy, too," he said.

***

Tuesday was more unsettling than the first day back. Not because more blood was spilled on my behalf—quite the contrary. The adventure of Shoe Makinen and MaryAnne DuPree on the South Branch was no longer the novelty it had been just the day before. Like yesterday's headline, that was old news. Kids were talking about Jimmy and Mr. Saddelkamp getting their car stuck in the mud in front of Crossjaw's place, and how Mr. Crossjaw threatened the Saddlekamps to make it right or he would get even.

Some said the Saddlekamps were on the road, others sided with the Crossjaws, who claimed that the storekeeper turned around in the driveway, spinning unsightly ruts into what was rightfully theirs. I didn't see how it mattered.

All of the Crossjaw boys were conveniently absent so Jimmy carried the day, the only side of the story to be told, evident by the huddle of boys pressing him between classes.

I was relieved that the limelight was off of me, but unsettled by the fact that MaryAnne was absent a second day in a row. I spent class time wondering how I might uncover her excuse for being out of school, but still had not conceptualized a plan as I shuffled home, stopping at puddles along the way, cracking ice at the water's edge with my heel. A boot imprint that caught my attention brought back the recollection of tracks left by Gaspard at Mrs. Krebbs' place. I decided to swing by.

Approaching the place gingerly, I checked over my shoulders to be sure I was alone. No new disturbances appeared in the yard, except for multiple tire tracks where grass met the dirt road. Sheriff Downing, I presumed, patrolling the place. The house, abandoned once again, looked dark and cold. *Gaspard must have caught wind that we were on to him*, I thought. Perhaps he got distracted with the news of his long-lost brother and skipped town to search for the wretched hermit instead of pursuing my friend. Whatever the cause, I was glad he was gone, so that Mrs. Krebbs' home could rest in peace.

***

"Where have you been?" I asked as I gently tugged MaryAnne's elbow before class the following day. My heart leapt when I saw a wisp of auburn hair through the crowded hallway so I scurried to catch up, allowing my hand to linger a moment on the soft wool of her coat. MaryAnne turned on her heel.

"Oh, hi, Shoes."

I took note that her coat was as clean as the day it was new. She was put together, every hair in place and a bright spark in her eye. Quite the contrast from our last moments together.

"Were you sick?" I asked.

"No. Mom and I spent some time together. It was good."

"So, no trouble at home after . . . all of what happened?"

MaryAnne smiled at Becky as she passed by, then waited for others to clear. When they didn't, she signaled to a corner by the radiator beneath the only window in the hallway. Out of earshot of the others prepping for class, I leaned against the wall and crossed my legs. MaryAnne held her books out for me to hold, then warmed her hands and continued.

"Things are good at home. After what happened last week, I think I love my mom and dad more than ever, realizing what they did for me." MaryAnne gazed through the window at an overcast sky. "Me and Mom talked about things we never talked about before. It's like we got to know each other for the very first time. I didn't know what I was missing." MaryAnne directed her gaze at me. "Is that how it is with you and your dad, growing up with him all your life? Is it like you have this special thing together?

I uncrossed my legs and fanned the pages of her geography book.

"I don't think so," I said. "Your family isn't like ours. I mean—I'm not talking about you being adopted. Not that. You and your mom have something different—even your dad." I struggled with how to say what I wanted to say to MaryAnne. The case that I had been on, trying to figure her out, wasn't going to be solved without confronting her about it. As much as MaryAnne intrigued me, I was weary of the mystery that made up her being. The more I got to know my friend, the less I understood her—her resilience, her joy when it made little sense. Having discovered the truth of MaryAnne's past only served to multiply my perplexity.

"Can I ask you something?" I said.

"Sure," MaryAnne said tentatively.

"You sound a lot like Mrs. Krebbs did."

One brow raised, as did the corner of her mouth. "That's not a question," said MaryAnne.

"How do you do it?" I asked. "What makes you so . . . you're so sweet."

She smiled, embarrassed.

"How can you go from finding out that you're not who you thought you were, to forgiving your adoptive parents—who lied to you—and now you love them even more?! You're a mystery to me, MaryAnne!"

MaryAnne bit back a gentle smile. "You really want to know, don't you."

"Y-e-eah!" I said with annoyance.

The starting bell rang sharply through my response, bringing our conversation to a close. MaryAnne took her books from me.

"I'll tell you after school—on the walk home?"

I nodded in acceptance and watched as she walked away, wondering what I was in for.

***

By lunchtime, the sun had broken through to warm the south side of my maple where I found solitude to eat, apart from Axel two days before. I sat down at the trunk of the tree, on a patch of brown grass, a small oasis amid the wet, cold ground of spring. My mind drifted swiftly to a greater place of solitude . . . I missed checking my traps, the adrenaline of a catch, the disappointment of a frozen set, the independent strategy to greater success. A cold, humid breeze brought me back to that place of quiet, the rush of clear water over a dam, absent of people and problems—that was, before last week. I basked as the sun warmed my face, eyes closed . . .

"Shoes."

I awakened out of my daydream to the sight of MaryAnne and Buffalo Alice. Buffalo locked on me, sternly. Ample yardage of coat cloth swayed as she drew to a halt.

"Shoes," MaryAnne said with an air of formality, "I would like you to meet my new sister-to-be, Alice Hawthorne." MaryAnne gestured a dainty hand and looked up at Buffalo. "Or should I say, Alice DuPree?" she asked sweetly.

It was timely that I wasn't swallowing lunch at that moment, because the gasp I took might have blocked my airway, and any life remaining in me as I sagged against the trunk of the tree.

"Makinen!" Buffalo snorted.

"You can call him Shoe, Alice."

"Shoe," Buffalo echoed.

I got to my feet—they were girls, after all. MaryAnne cocked her head at me, expectantly. "Shoes . . ."

I breathed two deep breaths, working up what needed to be said.

"Hi, Alice."

It pained me to say that. Calling Alice by her given name was like ceding a line of defense, capitulating on the stronghold taken against the girl by every other boy at Stoney Creek School. How weak had I become? Yielding to MaryAnne, addressing Alice as who she really was, and having to uphold my integrity from this day forth before MaryAnne and the whole school.

"You'd better have something good," I said to her as she returned an inquisitive look back at me. "On our walk home . . . remember?"

"Oh, yes." MaryAnne glanced up to Alice and back at me. "All friends now?"

I could see from the corner of my eye that Alice wasn't looking my way and I was loath to lay eyes on her. "Yup," we muttered in unison.

***

"I still wonder about them," MaryAnne sighed as we started on the road home.

"Them?"

"All the time. My birth father . . . my uncle."

"Why?"

"They're family." MaryAnne looked at me as I watched the road. "As disgusting as it might sound to you, Shoes, they're both a part of who I am."

"But Snuffy? You care about Clem Ruskin?"

"I don't care if I ever see him again. I'd rather not, in fact! I only meant that I think about both of them because, as far as I know, they are the only blood relatives I have, the only ones I've ever seen. Or should I say, Clem is the only one I've seen."

"Forget them," I said, ". . . if you can."

"I don't know if that's possible, Shoes."

"Yeah." I wanted to change the subject, to hear MaryAnne's secret, especially after witnessing her special treatment of Alice.

"So, Mrs. Krebbs . . . tell me how you do it."

"Shoes, don't call me Mrs. Krebbs. She was a sweet lady, but she wasn't anything like me!"

"You two sound a lot alike."

"I think the only thing we had in common was the Lord," said MaryAnne, "if that's what you mean."

I listened while kicking one stone ahead of me as we walked.

"I used to be a brat."

"Really?"

"Well, a lost brat—that's worse. When we lived in Menasha—that's in Wisconsin," MaryAnne explained.

I was glad she did, for Menasha was as foreign to me as an exotic jungle on the other side of the world.

"When we lived there, Sara died suddenly from a high fever. She was my best friend. Nobody thought it would happen, especially me. I was scared about dying after that. I had nightmares about it and was real worried that if it happened to me, where would I go? Have you ever thought about that?"

Of course I had, but I wasn't going to tell MaryAnne. Those kind of thoughts were fleeting, anyway. Even though I'd dodged Snuffy's bullets and had more scrapes than most boys my age, I didn't imagine death was near the door, and old age was a long way off. I chose to leave the fear of death for the girls.

"Not really," I said.

"Well, I did. I was nine—almost ten. I was scared, and I was tired of doing bad things."

"Like what?"

"Like breaking Mom's favorite vase and lying about it; blaming Mom for anything that didn't go my way. One time I took a penny from Dad's trousers and then bought a candy stick with it when Mom wasn't looking. It was the worst candy I ever ate, tasted like guilt."

"You did all that?"

"That and more. But I won't bore you with it. That was me before Jesus."

MaryAnne skipped in front of me to kick the stone, but I beat her to it.

"Hey!" She bumped my shoulder in jest.

"I don't think I would have liked you then," I said.

"*I* didn't like me then." MaryAnne reflected, "Dad was working late one night and Mom and I had dinner alone. Mom sent me to my room for complaining about helping with the dishes. I didn't stay there where I should have. Instead, I snuck into the water closet for no reason. I looked in the mirror, disgusted with my hair. I hated my red hair. I was mad at Mom. I didn't like what was in the mirror, so I slapped it. Kinda dumb, I know, but that's what I did, and the mirror crashed in a thousand pieces on the floor."

"Wow."

"Mom found me bawling in my room." MaryAnne chuckled. "I told her why I hit the mirror. Then, with the softest voice, she told me how I was a special creature, made in God's image. That what I saw in the mirror was bearing God's image. And she said I should talk to him about it."

"To God?"

"Yeah," MaryAnne said.

"Just like that? Talk to God?"

"That's what *I* thought. But I did. I just talked to God about all the things I didn't like about my mom and dad, and then about myself. And somehow—it was like he shined a light inside me—what I was really saying to God about the things I didn't like—they were all my own sins! Before I knew it, I was telling God I was sorry for all that stuff. It took a while, because there was a lot to be sorry for, but when I was done, Jesus took me. I'm telling you, Shoes, Jesus lives in me. He couldn't before because of all the junk on my heart. But now he does."

I listened. Uneasily.

"After that, I hated lying. It was the first thing that changed in me. I wanted to tell the truth all the time. I wanted to tell everyone else how they should be telling the truth too, but I had to bite my tongue—that was hard for me."

"I bet," I said.

"I think Mom and Dad were very relieved when I stopped lying. Other things changed, too. Once I took my eyes off myself, I started to look at others differently. Like Alice. She doesn't know it yet, but she bears God's image. Alice hasn't been treated well, and I want to be a good sister to her, even if she is a bully sometimes."

"Sometimes?!"

"Give her a chance, Shoes."

"So that's it? You prayed a prayer and then you suddenly changed into . . . sweet MaryAnne?"

"Well, not exactly. I'm not perfect, you know. Sometimes I still frown at my hair," MaryAnne said, with one dimple for me.

"You shouldn't do that," I said. "Your hair is fine."

"I know—I'm stuck with it anyway." MaryAnne laughed aloud. "The difference now is, I want to do good in God's sight, because of what he already did for me. That's it."

My ears listened, but my head didn't fully comprehend. I had hoped for something more profound, something more than a prayer in MaryAnne's bedroom. Still, she sounded so confident in her story, nothing remained for me to question. It was hers. And somehow, I knew MaryAnne was telling me about a part of her that no one could take away. For me the mystery was solved, at least for the time being. The different girl who entered my fifth grade was different because of something between her and God. Strange, in a way, but a strange that was growing on me.

I kicked the rock hard so that it came to a stop past the far edge of the Co-op. MaryAnne darted ahead.

"Race ya!" she said with glee.

Taken by surprise, I trailed three steps behind, then suddenly stopped in my tracks. Far down the road, from the outskirts of town came a familiar, dark figure. My body stiffened, for there was no mistaking that gaunt frame and the unusual black sport coat.

MaryAnne passed the Co-op, stepped on the stone, and spun around.

"Beat ya!" MaryAnne bantered. "Hey! You didn't even try!"

I sprinted to her and leaned in with a loud whisper, "There he is."

"Who?" MaryAnne looked over her shoulder.

"Gaspard. We need to get outta here." I nudged MaryAnne toward the alley to my house, a change of plans to divert her from the road to her home and away from Gaspard Ruskin. MaryAnne followed me into the alleyway, then hesitated.

"Wait a minute," she said. "This is my chance."

"What?"

MaryAnne postured with determination, "I've never seen my birth father—this might be my only chance to meet him."

"MaryAnne!" I glared a threatening glare. "Let's go to my house. Trust me, he's creepy!"

MaryAnne bit her lip in contemplation, then turned back to the main road.

"MaryAnne!" I hissed.

She ignored me and started up the road toward her home as if nothing was amiss. Given no choice but to follow, I caught up to her in a few long strides. Gaspard meandered toward us, directly ahead, as we neared the edge of town.

I whispered angrily, "Okay, now you've seen him. Let's turn around."

MaryAnne didn't listen. Hands in her coat pockets, she confidently approached the guy as if about to greet a newcomer at church. I did my best to put on an air of confidence, like my friend.

"Hi," she said as the man approached.

He closed the gap between us, halted, and stared at MaryAnne through tranced, droopy eyes. A chill shot down my spine. Then Gaspard Ruskin, with the fullness of unemotional detachment, opened his mouth to speak.

"Mildred," he said.

16

Apprehended

"**M**y name is MaryAnne." MaryAnne reached out her delicate hand in friendly greeting. Gaspard gave her the cold, limp handshake I vividly recalled from our first encounter.

"It's been a long time," her birth father droned. MaryAnne retracted, but Gaspard held her hand fast. "How's my girl been?"

"F-f-fine," she said, cocking her head.

"We're running kinda late," I lied, "so we have to get going."

The man didn't even look at me.

"What's the hurry?" he asked as he gazed through MaryAnne, then cupped her hand in both of his large, gnarled paws. "Why don't you come with me? You and I have a lot to catch up on."

MaryAnne looked at me, startled.

"Where are you taking her?" I demanded to know.

Again, Gaspard ignored my voice, riveted on MaryAnne, then began to lead her the way he came, outside of Stoney Creek. MaryAnne followed, reluctantly, arm outstretched.

"Where are we going?" she worried.

"We're just takin' a little walk, you and I. Tell your friend to skedaddle. We won't be long."

"Let her go!" I yelled, following closely behind.

"Ow!" MaryAnne screamed, as Gaspard crushed her hand and pulled her closer.

"I said, let her go!" With that, I shoved Gaspard between the shoulder blades with all the force I could muster. He stumbled, hands locked on MaryAnne, and spun around.

"If you know what's good for the girl, Mac, you'll leave us alone. We have some visitin' to do, and everything'll be fine." Gaspard's trance had changed to a mean scowl. "Don't do anything stupid," he said.

I froze in a moment of indecision. Without a weapon up my sleeve or a dead beaver in a sack, I had nothing to combat the tyrant with. I looked around for something in desperation, to no avail. Gaspard was lanky, but certainly not weak, judging by his quick recovery from my blow to his back. His grip on MaryAnne was fast, and I had no reason to second-guess his threat on her. MaryAnne kept pleading at me with her scared, blue eyes. Dad's words of wisdom returned to me, "You should have gotten help . . ."

With that, I mouthed, *I'll be back,* to MaryAnne, then bolted at top speed.

I covered the distance to our alley in record time, spinning dirt as I turned the corner. It was in front of Mrs. Krebbs' house that I realized only Mom, Ricky, and Sophie would be home. Dad and Mr. DuPree were still at work, along with nearly every other man in town. I reversed course to the Co-op in the hopes of finding Mr. Saddlekamp to assist. The entry bell on the door rang loudly as I barged through. Jimmy was at the counter, taking his shift after school.

"Where's your dad?!"

"Out for supplies. Why?"

"Call the sheriff. MaryAnne's being kidnapped!"

I stopped the door from closing, jumped from the porch landing over three steps and onto the road, then spun gravel toward the mill. I hadn't noticed my heart pounding in my chest until I reached the loading zone where Dad could be found with his wagon and team.

He was not there.

Mr. Johnson operated the saw while Mr. DuPree loaded an empty wagon.

"STOP!" I yelled.

Mr. Johnson reeled at the cry of my voice over the screaming saw. He glared at me with a mixture of alarm and anger as he pulled a lever, retracting a log from the whirring blade. Mr. DuPree met me, grabbing my shoulders.

"What is it, Arthur?"

"MaryAnne. Gaspard's got her!"

Mr. DuPree let me go in an instinctive reaction to leave, then turned back.

"Where?"

"North of town, close to your house!" I said, racing him out of the mill entrance to where I had last seen MaryAnne. Mr. DuPree overtook me as I gasped to keep up. Never had I witnessed a dad run with such speed as Mr. DuPree, in a life-and-death pursuit for his daughter. The agility with which he carried his powerful body spurred me to maintain a close following distance, despite the sensation that my lungs were about to burst.

Past the Co-op on the north side of town, I spied a road clear of pedestrians and the distinct radiator of Mr. Saddlekamp's Chevy coming our way. Mr. DuPree flagged him down.

"Adrien," Mr. Saddlekamp said as he braked to a stop. "What can I do for you?"

"It's MaryAnne. She's been taken by Clem's brother," Mr. DuPree said between breaths. "Did you see anyone on the road back there?"

"Just a lanky fella all alone, headin' out of town."

"Can you take us?"

"Hop in!"

Mr. DuPree ran around to the front seat as I struggled for position in the back amongst boxes, three flour bags, and a stack of new gunny sacks.

"Find room back there?" asked Mr. Saddlekamp. "Needed a few supplies from Maple Hill for the Co-op before the next truck shows up."

I nestled in and pulled the door hard against my side until it clicked. Mr. Saddlekamp sped off. We rumbled along the bumpy road for no more than a minute or two when the distinct figure of Gaspard came into view through the car's front glass.

"That's him!" I said.

Mr. Saddlekamp slowed. Gaspard extended his arm and held out a thumb at the sight of our approaching vehicle.

"Looks like we've got ourselves a hitchhiker," said Mr. Saddlekamp.

"Get down, Arthur," said Mr. DuPree. "He'll recognize you."

There was no place to get down *to*. I grabbed a gunny sack, covered my lap, quickly pulled another over my head, then slunk until my knees jammed the driver's seat in front of me. Just another sack of goods, I hoped. The car rolled to a stop.

"Where you headed?" said Mr. DuPree.

A muffled response came from outside the car, just audible over the clamor of the auto's engine.

"Up the road to the next town."

"You alone?"

"Me and my girl. Mildred! Git up 'ere!"

"Wait, Adrien," I heard Mr. Saddlekamp whisper. "Let her get closer."

I wanted to tear the sack off my head to see what was about to play out, but restrained myself so as to not blow our cover.

"We're a bit tight," said Mr. DuPree. "Let me make some room for you in the back seat." The click of a car door was followed by the sound of boots on the gravel road.

"Daddy!" MaryAnne cried.

What happened next could only be described as the sound of a bone-crushing blow on raw flesh. I ripped the burlap sack from my head, then in a single motion, opened the car door and fell to the ground amidst the sound of scuffles and groans.

Mr. Saddlekamp exited his door just as I rounded the back of the car to find Mr. DuPree in the throes of one last blow to Gaspard's blood-stained face, knocking him out cold. MaryAnne shuddered at my side, hand over her mouth.

"Are you okay?"

She nodded, choking back tears.

"I'm sorry he got away with you like that."

MaryAnne shook her head. "I should have listened!" she sobbed.

"James! Got any rope in there?" Mr. DuPree rolled Gaspard onto his face and pulled one hand high up on the man's back. Mr. Saddlekamp rustled through his collection of items in the car, then came up with a length of bailing twine and handed it to MaryAnne's father. Mr. DuPree bound Gaspard's wrists tight and high.

"That's going to hurt when he comes to," said Mr. Saddlekamp.

"Not any more than the lick I gave him on his kisser," remarked Mr. DuPree, shaking his right hand in pain as he got to his feet.

The tall, dark-haired father of MaryAnne was a man I held in high regard—and fearful reverence at times. I equally admired his powerful physique. Witnessing him demonstrate his strength in finest valor left me awestruck. He reached for MaryAnne and swept her up in his arms as if she were a feather lilting to the side of the road.

"Are you okay, my sweetheart?" MaryAnne buried her face in her father's neck, whispering something as she squeezed his throat tight. "I love you, too, honey. Thank the good Lord you're fine," he wheezed, then propped her on her feet.

A growing rumble from town demanded our attention as another auto approached at high speed. I backed off as the county sheriff's car skidded to a stop behind Saddlekamp's Chevy. Sheriff Downing struggled out of the vehicle, then groaned to his feet.

"Got a call that there's been some trouble here," he said over the roof of the Ford.

"Not anymore, Sheriff," said Mr. Saddlekamp.

"What can I do for you then?" the sheriff asked as he closed his car door and stepped between both autos.

"We caught you a rascal that was trying to steal my daughter," said Mr. DuPree, signaling toward Gaspard, still facedown on the shoulder. "You showed up in the nick of time. We're kind of short on space, and we were hoping you could give this fella a ride before he comes to."

The sheriff gaped at the lifeless body.

"Perhaps a room that's a little more comfortable than the roadside—with a solid lock and key?" said Mr. DuPree.

"Hmph," said Sheriff Downing, standing watch over the apprehended criminal. The sheriff unclipped a pair of handcuffs from his belt, snapped them over the twine on Gaspard's wrists, then rolled the body over, face-up. Sand, small stones, and a blade of last year's grass adhered to the thickening blood on Gaspard's face.

"What did you do to him?!" asked the sheriff.

"Just settled a little dispute over what was rightfully mine," said MaryAnne's father.

"Looks like you got the best of him," said Sheriff Downing as he felt Gaspard's neck for a pulse. The sheriff shook his head at the unconscious man, then back to Mr. DuPree. "Well then, help me get him in the car," he said. "He'll need a bit of mending when he comes to."

"Come on, Arthur," said Mr. DuPree. "Lift one of his legs."

Skinny as Gaspard was, I didn't realize how heavy a limp leg could be. The four of us wrestled MaryAnne's birth dad into the back seat of the sheriff's vehicle and slammed the door shut.

"You in on this again, Makinen?" the sheriff asked.

"Not much, sir. I mean, I tried to stop him, sir."

Sheriff Downing scrutinized me as if inspecting a subordinate's uniform. "I don't know if you're a magnet for trouble or the makings of a fine deputy someday."

"Yes, sir. I don't know, sir."

"Well, stay out of trouble. Can you try to do that, son?"

"Yes, sir," I said.

Sheriff slapped me on the back, then ambled to the other side of his car and gripped the handle of the driver's door. "I'll bring him in, but I'll be back—going to need depositions from each of you."

Mr. Saddlekamp nodded. Then we watched as the sheriff turned his car around and drove away.

"Shall we?" Mr. Saddlekamp signaled toward his Chevy.

The men got in front, MaryAnne separating them—a delicate petal pressed between two oversized shoulders. And I snuggled up with . . . burlap sacks.

17

Family Ties

MaryAnne's mother was beside herself when we arrived, unable to speak between sobs. She held her daughter in a quiet embrace while the rest of us looked on. Dad and Mom had arrived at MaryAnne's moments earlier, with Ricky and Sophie in tow. They came to check on Mrs. DuPree after Dad received word that MaryAnne had been kidnapped. Dad wanted to know exactly what happened as he held one hand around Mom's shoulder.

"MaryAnne insisted on saying hello to Gaspard, even though I urged her not to. When Gaspard pulled on her arm to take her away, I rammed him in the back, but he didn't let go. I thought of what you said, Dad, that I should get help. So that's when I ran to find you at the mill. When you weren't there, me and Mr. DuPree ran as fast as we could to where I saw MaryAnne last, and then Mr. DuPree flagged down Mr. Saddlekamp. I'm sure glad they were there 'cause I don't know what would have happened to

MaryAnne if her dad didn't teach that Gaspard guy a lesson!"

"You did good, son." Dad's face broke into a generous smile. "You did real good."

He pulled me by the sleeve, then wrapped his arm around me and squeezed tight. Mom followed suit, and suddenly we were in a three-way hug. I closed my eyes to soak in the moment until Ricky attempted a chin-up on Dad's elbow, while Sophie yanked on Mom's dress. In a moment of awkward awareness, I glanced over my shoulder at the DuPrees, gawking at us with sweet smiles like they had never seen such a thing. Ricky finally broke Dad's arm free just as Mrs. DuPree recovered to her familiar role of hostess.

"Why don't we all go in for a cup of coffee and rest our feet, shall we?"

The others passed through the welcoming DuPree entry while I lagged outside to ponder newly scrawled words on the door header, printed in elegant calligraphy. "*Enter ye in at the strait gate . . .*"

"Are you coming, Shoes?" asked MaryAnne.

In all of her struggle, mere minutes from a life in danger, MaryAnne was still there to see me welcomed to her door.

"This is a strait gate?" I asked.

MaryAnne looked quizzically, then glanced above her head.

"Oh, Dad asked Mom to write that on there—she has the most beautiful handwriting."

"But what does that mean—the strait gate?"

"Skinny. Like a narrow passage," she said nonchalantly.

I gauged the frame of the door, touching each side with my fingertips while MaryAnne waited before my open arms. *No different than ours*, I thought.

"Not *this* door, Shoes. Remember when I said that Jesus lives in me? That's what it means. The narrow gate is Jesus. C'mon, let's go in."

The smell of coffee and the lingering aroma of something baked that day greeted my nostrils as we entered the kitchen, where the men were engaged in serious conversation.

"He'll know where to find us. Besides, Downing's got my number here," said Mr. DuPree as we made our way through.

MaryAnne whispered, "Let's sit in the front room."

My heart leapt at the opportunity to visit quietly with my best friend. I longed to see her dimples, to hear her laugh again, in the undisturbed quiet of the DuPree home, where peace seemed to roam freely while the cares of the world remained safely outside. I followed her red tress, tousled from the day's events, as she entered the solitude of the front room.

"Have a seat!" MaryAnne said breezily as she lighted on the davenport—beside Alice.

My longing gaze fell to the floor as my heart sank into the pit of my stomach. Alice caught MaryAnne in both arms and enveloped her with a strong hug that alerted my protective instincts. I settled in a side chair only after Alice let her go and the two sat chummy together on the couch.

"Hi, Alice," I said. It was the least I could do for MaryAnne.

"Shoe," retorted Alice, then turned to MaryAnne. "He didn't hurt you, did he?"

"Who?"

"Makinen! . . . Just kidding!" Alice roared with delight, scaring all peace from the DuPree home to a safe haven somewhere far across the county line. "Mom told me—is it okay that I call our mom 'Mom'?"

MaryAnne smiled, nodding briskly.

"Mom told me about Gaspard—he didn't hurt you, did he?"

"I'm okay, Alice. He didn't do anything." MaryAnne's eyes got lost in thought.

"Well, no one's gonna hurt you now that you've got me as your big sis!" declared Alice.

"I'm so glad you like it here," said MaryAnne. "Shoes, remember when I said you were lucky to have Ricky as a brother, and I wished I had a sister?"

"Yeah."

"That's what I was praying for all this time, and look what God did—he brought me a sister I never would have *dreamed* of!"

Neither would have I.

"Who would have thought?" MaryAnne continued. "When you and I were hiding in the bushes, watching Alice close the door as the police took her parents."

"You what?" Alice boomed. "You were there that night?!"

MaryAnne nodded.

"I was in my pajamas!" thundered Alice. I wondered what the big people were thinking about our conversation after that outburst.

"Yes, you were," MaryAnne giggled. "It's okay, we're sisters now," she said with glee. Then MaryAnne whispered loudly, "And Shoe is just like family." MaryAnne spied me, her dimples easing my disappointment.

There it was again, the kind heart that was uniquely MaryAnne, mirrored in her mother and Mrs. Krebbs. I couldn't take my eyes off of her. Witnessing MaryAnne discover who she really was only served to magnify her beauty in my eyes, as she reached beyond herself to others. What attracted me to her had grown beyond her delicate frame, the striking red hair, the joy on her face. MaryAnne's beauty shined through her eyes from somewhere within—a refinement unmatched. An allurement so pure. An attraction I was sure would never fade with time. I was "just like family" she had said. I found myself daydreaming for a time when that might come true.

Suddenly, Alice startled me from my dreamy thoughts, wresting my attention away with her big, toothy grin.

"Yeah, Makinen, now we're just like one big, happy family!"

THE END

Epilogue

Kids never looked at MaryAnne the same. Her kidnapping exposed the fact that MaryAnne was born a Ruskin. The news spread through Stoney Creek like wildfire through dry tinder in a pine forest. By the starting bell of the next school day, MaryAnne was looked upon as an outlaw by many, and as a Crossjaw by others. Funny how she didn't seem fazed. Her ill-treatment irked me, raising an instinct from deep within to fight for MaryAnne a time or two. I didn't. There was no need to. MaryAnne was amply protected by her new big sister, Alice.

Following our foray into Snuffy's territory, I never looked at MaryAnne the same way either. Her remarkable honor toward her parents, the kindness she showed Alice, and her quiet spirit—alive in the spunk that defined MaryAnne—riveted me.

We remained close friends. However, our friendship changed forever. Where once I felt free to share anything with her, there was something about our relationship that MaryAnne couldn't know. Not now.

Truth be told, I was stunned.

Dear Reader,

I hope you enjoyed *Mystery of MaryAnne*. I love to hear your feedback, so tell me what you liked, what you loved, even what you hated. You can write me at **DavidDeVowe@gmail.com.**

Also, I would like to ask you a favor. If you're so inclined, I'd really appreciate an honest review of *Mystery of MaryAnne*. If you have a moment, please go to my website, **DavidDeVowe.com**, and click on "Give a Book Review." It will take you to my author page where you can select this book for your review.

Thank you so much for reading and for spending time with Shoe and his friends.

In His Visible Hand,
David DeVowe